The Fug_tive Three

MIKE JENKINS

Cinnamon Press
Independent Innovative International

Published by Cinnamon Press
Meirion House, Glan yr afon, Tanygrisiau, Blaenau Ffestiniog
Gwynedd LL41 3SU www.cinnamonpress.com

The right of Mike Jenkins to be identified as author of this work has been asserted by him in accordance with the Copyright, Designs and Patent Act, 1988. © 2008 Mike Jenkins
ISBN 978-1-905614-46-2
British Library Cataloguing in Publication Data. A CIP record for this book can be obtained from the British Library

Designed and typeset in Palatino by Cinnamon Press
Cover design by Mike Fortune-Wood from original artwork: 'Graffiti' by Paul Maguire, agency: dreamstime.com. Printed and bound in Great Britain by Biddles Ltd, King's Lynn, Norfolk.
The publisher acknowledges the financial support of the Welsh Books Council

Acknowledgements:

Thanks to Academi for a bursary that assisted in the writing of this novella.
Lines quoted from Emily Dickinson: 'The heart asks pleasure first/And then, excuse from pain-' and 'The privilege to die.' are from *Complete Poems*, 1924, Part One: Life IX and 'Doom's electric Moccasin' from *Complete Poems*, 1924, Part One: Life XXVI, The Storm.

The Fugitive Three

Shell. Empty. A single shell on a beach. She'd been there once, Porthcawl. The oily sand underfoot had threatened to suck her in.

Shells. Her mam's empty syringes scattered. Those eyes and the eyes of her friends. Might as well be dead. Yet it was the longest escape. And where could she go now?

A teacher had said... She remembered him. He was different. Not a wanker like most of them, but friendly, even if he had dog's-breath. He'd said it was a poet's name. Bit of a rebel, like her. Didn't believe in God, things like that.

She watched from her window as people passed by on their way downtown. Dressed in party gear, even though it was a chilly April evening. Saturday and nowhere to go. Saturday made it worse. Even in the homes they'd gone on trips, bowling or to the pictures. Now all these pubbers and clubbers going past, dressed like birds of paradise, made her feel all the more depressed.

Tomorrow the rent, and she'd finished in her job. 'Laid off' they called it in the factory, but she knew better. She was 'casual' and they'd never have her back. How could she tell Ray Gun? That was his nickname, but where did it come from? She'd rather not find out.

Mary picked up her mother's photo from the dresser. She gave it a kiss and whispered to it –

'Mam, don worry. It'll be orright. I'm shewer ee's a good boy. Ee sayz I'm special.'

Her mam smiled back. She wished she'd learnt to smile like that. Instead, she had somehow copied her father's straight-faced expressions which gave nothing away. Apart from that, they'd been like sisters; her mam so open. A great listener, everyone said. She wished she could meet her ghost. Mary had tried hard enough. Lying on the bed, putting on her clothes, rubbing her rings to make the genie appear. But it never did. Her father had found her once, in her mam's nightgown. Thought she'd gone mad. He swore at her and that wasn't like him.

He was already out. Some dinner with the Masons. When she was young she thought it was a pub; the Masons' Arms. Now she knew better. Her dad specialised in secrets. It had been years before Mary found out his first name, Frank. Her mam always addressed him as 'dad'.

She felt small in the spacious house, as though she'd shrunk to a child while talking to her mam's image. Her ears strained for the phone and Ant's voice to bring her back to the present, to give her a sense of purpose on an empty evening.

Sam burst into his wreck of a room like a hurricane, treading on a discarded chip carton.

'This place is a fuckin tip!'

As if it belonged to somebody else. From the next bedroom his brother John's electric guitar was a baby being tortured.

'Shut the fuck up, Endrix, or ooever yew are!' he yelled, but the smoke-yellow wallpaper never answered. Instead, it got worse, and there was a cat being strangled by chicken-wire.

Sam had to get something for his head. It was a building-site where workmen drilled all day long.

'It's somewhere! It's gotta be somewhere!'

He ransacked his room, pulling out drawers, lifting old socks and shaking them.

'Where the ell did I ide it?'

He swooped under the bed like a police-diver after evidence. He hauled out a couple of porn mags and leafed through them.

'Don know why I bother! If ee's ad it!'

Sam whirled. Pounded on the wall. No effect. Rushed to his brother's. Broke in. Miming words like a fish just hooked, as John pressed the electrodes to his temples, increased the pain.

Sam pulled the plug on him.

'What the f…!'

'Did yew skank it, or wha?'

'What yew on bout?'

'The tenner, tha's what I'm on bout. My fuckin tenner!'

Shelly could smell gas, she was sure she could. The dilapidated stove in the corner of her bed-sit. The window had a gap-tooth. The gas would never get her. Unless she lit a match to try. Blew it all up in one gesture. Who'd notice the difference?

'If I woz in a soap-opera, they'd kill me off in a first episode, she thought, ave me jumpin off of the Arches or summin.'

She chuckled to herself, not knowing where her sense of humour came from. Kay had helped her, no doubt. Her care worker. Shelly even felt she had belonged to her. Her second mother. She wanted so much, because her own couldn't cope.

The stream of down-town youngsters lapsed to a trickle. She recognized a couple from school: chocolate boy Anthony Pearson and this girl who really fancied herself, Leanne something.

Shell thought about following them, cadging a drink.

She couldn't stay in this hole; it was colder and damper than the streets outside. They wouldn't recognize her though, a face who'd come and gone from school.

'Yewr goin to do summin Shelly Bush. I don't care what anyone else says. Yew've got starry eyes!'

And according to Kay, "starry eyes" was a very rare condition. Shell put it down to too much skunk in the air when she was little.

She clinked the change in her jeans' pocket. Her jeans were a disgrace, fraying at the bottom. If only her mam's beloved punk came back into fashion...

The trickle ended. She'd be a droplet. Maybe a tear shed. In Cwmtaff drizzle, it was all one.

The phone rang and Mary flung herself out of the room, knocking a history text-book from her desk. She hurtled downstairs as if it was a ski-slope.

Breathless when she lifted the receiver, 'Hiya!' she greeted.

'Can I speak to Frank, please?'

'Oh yeah... I mean, no... sorry, ee isn't in.'

It was a woman. Probably one from his firm's office.

'Sorry to bother you. Mary, isn't it?'

'Yeah! Can I take a message? He's at the Masons.'

She didn't want to sound too upset.

'Have I interrupted something?'

Heavy breathing. Hold it in. Mary thought of her insinuation.

'No, I woz jest expectin a call, tha's all. I'm in a rush!'

'Okie-dokie! Maybe I'll see you some time. Have a lovely evening.'

"Okie-dokie"? Who on earth says that kind of thing? When could she possibly see Mary? Was her dad actually meeting this woman?

She was confused and angry that it hadn't been her Ant. He was from the estate, but he was academic. The teachers said he was the exception. They spoilt him because he was from there. Whereas, it was supposed to be easy for her. She hovered by the phone, glaring at it. She soon began to loathe its neat, square numbers and signs. It was half past eight. She began to make excuses for him. His disabled father had taken a turn for the worse and been rushed to hospital. He'd been kept late at his Saturday job.

'I'll phone from the Club about eight.'

It was only half an hour, but she began to fear the worst. For someone who couldn't summon the spirits, she did have powerful feelings when things weren't right.

'Ant, c'mon! C'mon, I carn stand it!' She urged the stubborn object.

'Stuff yewr tenner, Sam. I int got it an anyway, I wouldn go near yewr room, I might catch dysentery or summin.'

Sam could never fathom how they were brothers. John was so laid-back most of the time. His straggly hair covering his face, while Sam was all wiry energy.

'Well, it's fuckin gone, tha's all I know an I'm totelee broke. Do us a favour...'

But John ignored his brother and re-plugged his guitar. The crashing chords were two juggernauts hitting each other face on.

Sam swivelled and slammed the door shut. His mam was downstairs watching *Blind Date*. Her handbag would be next to her, below the chair. If only he could drug her up. Just for a couple of minutes. Not "date rape" but "handbag mug" drug. He contemplated wild stories to distract her – 'Mam, John's jest set fire to hisself with a spliff!' Not so wild maybe. Or – 'Mam, I found a colony o rats in my room. We gotta do summin quick!' Likely, but she would be too scared of the rodents.

Alternatively, he could go down and chat to her. That really would make her suspicious though. All he needed was twenty, max. Enough for a few jars and a couple of tab's, Es or speed, whatever. Saturday was passing him by and his friends would soon be down the Royal playing pool.

He went to the bathroom and doused his face in cold water. It didn't cure his headache, but brought some relief. He squirted toothpaste along his right index finger in the absence of a brush. He put it under tap-water and the toothpaste ran away, caterpillarring down the plug-hole.

'Shit!'

He decided to go downstairs, make a cuppa and hope for a moment to pounce. His mam didn't look up, but addressed him as he passed in front of her.

'Wha you doin, Sam? You never stays in on a Saturday evenin like.'

'Why? Wha's it t yew?'

'Oh, sorry I spoke.'

Sam had a problem finding the tea-bags. He shifted all the boxes in the cupboard and cursed.

'There's a map t the kitchen on the wall, love. You'll easy find you way round en.'

'Moany ol cow,' he muttered.

'Whaaa?'

His mam's Cardiff accent got on his nerves. She sounded like a crow. She must've been the only person ever to move from Cardiff up the Valleys. It was always the other way.

Eventually, he sorted the kettle, had the teapot ready and found a mug which wasn't decomposing. The doorbell rang and he was ready to act. With any luck it was his mam's friend Sarah, calling for a gossip.

'You get it, Sam!'

'Carn, I'm gettin a cuppa.'

'Oh, orright. I on'y bin workin all day long. Buh it don matter, like.'

Soon as she got up, he'd be on it. Like a buzzard on a field-mouse.

Shell brushed the knots out of her hair. It had a natural wave, but she always wanted to straighten it. Everything about herself made her discontented. She counted her fortune: £3.52 plus one French coin like a 5p piece. How was it whenever she was broke, there was inevitably a French coin? Perhaps she'd save them up and go to Paris. She wondered how much chewing-gum cost there.

She had difficulty locking her door. Ray Castleton, the landlord, had shown her. He'd steered her hands and breathed down her ear. She'd shrugged him off, but he still kept patting her bare arm. He wasn't the typical landlord. He looked like an aging hippy with hair in a pony-tail and multi-coloured waistcoats. When flares came back in he was supercool. He had a reputation. He'd even known Shell's mam. She'd have to be strong.

Shell ambled down High Street. A few of the pubs pounded, others were dark and silent places where drinking was a serious business. A stagger of lads was approaching her, their guffaws cuffing the streetlamps. She thought about crossing the road, but it was too late. She strode fast towards them, hoping they'd part.

Immediately, comments ambushed her –

'Ey, love, wha about it en?'

'On yewr own? Come with us, we'll entertain yew.'

They all launched into Robbie Williams' *Mr. DJ* and one tried to run up a lampost. Shell sighed, muttering after them, 'Fuckin wankers!'

She bought curry and chips and that was half her cash gone. She sat on a bench by the War Memorial. It was out of the way and safer. She loved the way the curry soaked into the chips. The spicy taste made her feel alive at last. She licked her lips.

Money, Money, Money… Abba's annoying song kept repeating in her head. The more she willed it to go, the more it revolved. She could go from bar to bar asking for work. There were too many hazards on a Saturday night. She contemplated easy crimes, but there weren't any. CCTV ruled the town now. She could hear her mam's mocking tones – 'Make yewr money on yewr back, Shelly. Yew might as well sell it, coz there's plenty'll want it f free!'

'Wanna sup?'

Shell jumped. A bloated man in his twenties was sitting on the other end of the bench. He offered her his can of lager. He dribbled and wiped his mouth with his sleeve, stuttering as he spoke.

'Uh… uh… uh… I'm… Clare… wh… wha's… yewr name then?'

She thought he'd said "Clare", but couldn't be certain. She got up to leave. He stood up too, mimicking.

'Clare!'

'Are yew? Yeah… uh… uh… I'm C… C… Clive. Pleased t meet yew!'

*

Mary gave up on the phone. She pulled it out of its socket. Maybe her dad was right about Ant after all. Maybe he was a waste of space. Though she wished he was wrong, because he was such a snob. Her mam would've understood.

'Whatever's good f yew, love. I do trust yew, but jest watch out tha's all. Most men're on'y out f what they cun get.'

She removed her make-up and changed into her nightie, abandoning the evening. She tried watching telly, but it was a boring chat-show. Even the music wouldn't play for her, the rousing chorus of *International Velvet* sounding obscene in her state of mind. She thought the worst. Ant in bed with someone else, some girl who gave him everything he wanted. She regretted being so restrained.

She scoured the house for remnants of her mother, touching the brolly in the hallway, smelling the lavender talc in the bathroom. It all led her to their bedroom. She entered into half-light. It was no longer a shrine. He'd cleared away most traces of her mam and would soon do the same for the rest of the house.

Mary lay on the left of the double-bed, her father's place. She curled up and put her thumb in her mouth, gently sucking it.

'Mam, mam, mam…' she intoned, 'oo cun I talk to without yew? Jest a word, jest one word is all I ask.'

She pictured her lying there, her smile to heal so much, 'Don worry, love. Yew'll always ave us.'

He couldn't find her purse. It was a Lucky Dip in his mam's handbag. There were elastic bands, brushes, but mostly hairs. You could make a couple of wigs from the insides. Eventually, he found a twenty and slid it out. She only had forty altogether, so she'd soon miss it. As he was still crouching, his mam and Sarah entered. He pretended to fall backwards, but it became all too real when he knocked into the telly, sending Cilla Black into a snowstorm!

'Wha's ee like, eh Sare?'

'What yew doin, Sam, avin a fit?'

Sam's hair spiked up, as if from an electric shock. He put on a totally disorientated act, getting up and jiggling his limbs about, testing they still functioned.

'No, Mrs Phillips... er... yeah... I seen this ewge spider an I woz chasin it outa room an...'

He put his hand in his pocket, scrumpling the twenty up in an old tissue. Sarah Phillips saw an over-excited eighteen year-old. His mam saw a complete idiot.

'Get a grip, Sam... look what you done t the telly. You goin t fix it like?'

Sam gawped at the TV. All things mechanical were mysteries to him.

'It's okay, Jean. It's the aerial. I know coz we ad the same problem evry time ower cat sat on the telly.'

Sam hopped awkwardly from foot to foot.

'Sam, you goin anywhere, coz me an Sare're watchin this video. Wha's it called now, Sare?'

'*Clockwork Orange*. I liked the look of it. Tha funny-looking man from them new adverts is in it. It could be a bit like *Toy Story*.'

Sarah Phillips gave the video to Jean to inspect, while she set about fixing the TV. Sam smirked and smothered his giggles. His mam put her feet up for the evening on a tattered pouffe kept for this purpose alone.

'Wha's so funny?'

'Nothin, I ope yew enjoy it.' He played with the note in his pocket. 'I'm off! See yew whenever.'

As Sam sped upstairs to get his trainers on, the two women made themselves comfortable.

'Why's ee keep fiddlin in is pocket, Jean?'

'Dunno! You problee turns im on!'

'Really?'

'Well, ee's that desperate!'

'Give over! Le's get this video on. I ope it's a good larf. I could do with one.'

Clive gripped Shelly's hand and wouldn't let go. She was slightly perturbed, though he did seem harmless enough. She knew conversation was the best survival weapon. She carefully withdrew her right hand, forcing a smile. She never liked smiling, it revealed her wonky teeth.

'Where d yew live Clive?'

He took another long swig from the can. His face was puffed up. She recognised its tell-tale flesh. A few of her mam's companions had shared that toady look.

'S... St. Martin's... I... uh... I'm on m... mm... medication. It don d... do me no g... g... good though... Uh... I eat grass. It's a lot b... better. Ever see a sick orse? I... I... I woz eatin some b'there when yew come.'

He indicated a patch of grass in the direction of the Court building.

St. Martin's mental hospital. Her mam went there eventually. It was an open place, the residents often round town. He wasn't threatening. Needed somewhere to go, someone to care.

'Yew shouldn be yer, y'know.'

'N... n... neither should yew. Th... Tha's why I come over. Y...yew need a bodyguard. Uh... I could do the job, no problem.'

She knew it was wrong to exploit him, but her instinct took over.

'Lissen, Clive. I got no money. I gotta pay the rent an I've lost my job. Any ideas?'

'Y... y... yew could try a bank! They got plenty... uh... I seen it. When I woz little I ewsed t g... go with m... m... my dad.'

It was pointless, she should've known better.

'Lissen, Clive, yew shouldn eat grass. It's bard f yew. Yew never know wha dogs've shat an pissed on it.'

'N... n... n... no, it's fine! I... uh... always check it first. It's... uh... a bit like frewt an veg. Y... yew eat tha, don yew? Well, insects do their stuff over it all-a t... time, don ey?'

Shell laughed, but she was still not certain about trusting him.

'Shull we go f... fr a walk? I know piles o good spots. D... drink? No, fair enough. Th... there's a blast furnace jest over the bridge.'

Shelly edged away. She gazed up the road to see if anyone else was around. She steeled her voice, not to sound anxious.

'Blast furnace, eh? Intrestin... I gotta go ome now, Clive. It's bin really nice speakin t yew.'

He moved in unison. His eyes didn't have a speck of aggression Shelly felt guilty leaving him.

'Another night, Clive. I'll be down yer eatin my chips. I'll see yew then, right?'

'Then w... we cun go see the ol blast furnace, eh?'

'Yeah, why not!'

He flapped and supped again and she turned away. As she reached High Street, she was glad of pubs spilling out their bodies, girls now as well as men. The noisy banter made her more secure. Crossing the road, she thought she spied Clive in a nearby car-park echoing her steps. She halted in a shop doorway. *Mobile Warehouse* read the sign, but the shop was blacked-out by roller-blinds like all the rest, except the empty or derelict ones, which were spreading like an infection.

The last thing she wanted to do was return to that cell. Condensation would've clouded the window by now. Her bones would be hollowed by the chill. She had enough for a half, but drinking alone was sad. Not only that, but it drew boys to you like dogs on heat.

The pub opposite did seem inviting. The juke-box played the Stereophonics' *More Life in a Tramp's Vest.* Wish she could borrow one! Somebody she knew could be standing at the bar. Then again, she could spend the whole drink fencing off remarks.

A figure was hovering at the car-park's entrance. She decided the pub would be a sanctuary, for a while at least.

In a car, her dad driving. A large, fancy limo fit for a ball. Ant next to her on the back seat, holding her hand, tickling it with one finger. Her mam at the front, hair long and shining, full of youth.

Her father needing to get to an appointment, a Council meeting. Putting his foot down, the engine growling and grating. Over the brim of the hill and down, like a roller-coaster.

Down, down, down. Faster, faster, faster.

'There's no need, Dad…'

Before she could finish, the road led to a jetty, water on either side. Her dad braked and Ant's hand flew from her. The passenger door jerked open and Ant was thrown out. She observed from mid-air as he sank into the water, around him the snapping jaws of crocodiles. She knew she should dive in, rescue him. She knew also, they'd both be slaughtered. On the edge of the jetty now, by the front of the car. She leaned over its black bonnet, to implore. Her father had gone. He was striding on to get to the meeting. Her mam had fallen asleep, or unconscious. She frantically tapped at the windscreen, like a bird beating against a window-pane.

'Mam! Wake up! Mam! It's Ant! I don know what t do about im!'

But here mam had a gaunt, wrinkled face and her hair had turned grey. The windscreen blurred and gave way to a crinkled ceiling. She heard the muffled voice of a woman and thought, for a moment, it was still a dream.

Then the light switched on pierced, her vision. Her dad's stern tone:

'Mary! What are you doing here?'

'What's the matter, Frank?'

She roused herself despite a desire to return, to see Ant swim clear to safety. As she stood up unsteadily, there was relief it had only been a dream.

'Sorry, Dad... I woz fed up... Ant never rang... I woz thinkin o mam all-a time.'

A woman with bright lipstick, sharp features, joined her dad at the door. Her father became overly formal to cover up the embarrassment.

'Mary, this is Mrs Lake... er... Dorothy. She's my new personnel manager. I was just showing her round the house.'

Dorothy. Dot. Mary couldn't visualize her as a Dot. More of a point. Showing her round the double-bed, more like.

'I did phone earlier just to check... I mean... the phone was unplugged for some reason.'

'Yeah... sorry... I'll leave yew.'

As she brushed past them, Dorothy extended a hand

for her to shake.

'Mary, I do hope everything's…'

She went to the bathroom, leaving them to despoil her mam's bed. How could he forget so readily? Not a year gone and another life planned out. They had never really been suited. Her mam able to express her emotions. Her dad so constipated, he'd need a dose of high-fibre compassion to remark one compliment. Mary was bewildered how they'd ever fallen in love in the first place. He was so sound, dependable, efficient. Like an exam paper. Was she becoming the same?

In the mirror, she endeavoured to mould her features into a different shape, making exaggerated expressions. But, she kept seeing her dad's thin lips pursing back at her, unable to expand. And she didn't want them any more.

Baggy trousers, ball room. Sam had sprayed so much Lynx on he smelt like a harem. If there was any night left after he'd spent it, he'd sleep at Milky's flat.

His mam would suspect him, but he'd deny it, of course. Blame John, who'd probably go out later to meet his so-called band down the Community. John was always broke as well, spending every penny on useless equipment. The next Manics, so they claimed. Wales had had it though, Sam knew that. It was last year's thing.

Into the Royal, there was a clash of voices and competing lights. A telly above the bar, but no sound. Some of the girls he knew were standing around drinking *Breezers*. Mandy, who he fancied, in a skirt which doubled as a belt. Their mixed perfumes almost bowled him over, despite the smoke-filled room. He breathed deep to get a drag. He'd cadge one later from his mates.

'Hiya Mand… Cath, Deb!'

'Hiya, Sam! Goin t Supercool arfter, is it?'

'Maybe, I dunno… Sorry I carn buy yew all a drink. Bit skint see. But I gotta new job up tha pie factree. I'll treat yew all then, right?'

He lied to impress Mandy. She did smile back at him, but returned to the huddle of her friends.

'See yew arfta then, Sam!'

It seemed like a promise, but he couldn't be sure. Her voice both irritated and attracted him. He couldn't work out this ambiguity. Other girls he either liked or disliked. With Mandy, it was different.

He squeezed his way to the bar, finding gaps like a centre going for the try-line. His slim body helped. Finally at the bar, he looked back at the pool table to check. They were there alright, but hadn't noticed him. Lefty shaping up a shot and taking ages, like a chess-player, then failing to pot.

Next to him was a girl he recognized from school. She'd spent a lot of time bunking though, whereas he'd turned up and played hell with the teachers. He couldn't remember her name, but had a notion she'd been meeting one of his friends in Year 9. She didn't acknowledge Sam and was too busy getting the barmaid's attention. She wasn't exactly dressed for Saturday night. She had rings in her eye-brows and ears and a brick-hard face. When the barmaid asked Sam what he wanted and ignored the girl, she turned on him.

'Ey! I wuz yer before yew!'

Sam raised two palms and shrugged.

'Okay, okay. No prob! Go ahead!'

She stared at him momentarily. Sam wondered if she did recall him. The school was so vast, so many kids in those same black uniforms. She only ordered a half and counted out her money warily to pay.

'Yer, wha's this? It's a frog coin! I carn accept this!' The barmaid held up a coin like a 5p piece. Sam could see the girl only had 2p left.

'Well, carn I ave a cheaper lager then?'

The barmaid smirked with a look of 'what yew doin yer, dosser?'

'Yer, ave this f Chrissake. It's on'y 5p What's the big deal?'

Sam did his gentleman act. The girl unexpectedly smiled. She had two crooked teeth which made her brick exterior crumble, revealing a different inside.

'Ta! I'll pay yew back some time.'

'Don be darft!'

'No, I'm serious. Yew didn ave t bother.'

'Tha's orright, I know what it's like t be skint.'

Mandy spotted Sam chatting up this scruffy girl by the bar. They were standing too close to each other for her liking and the girl smiled in such a familiar way. How could he be drawn to something like that, that couldn't afford a bar of soap?

Sam ordered his bottle of *Bud*, which was on offer at a quid. He said a swift goodbye to the girl, who didn't seem to know anyone there at all. He felt a buzz of excitement as he exchanged greetings with the boys: Lefty, Byron and Milky. The night ahead was all that mattered now. Pool was their easy-going warm-up. He forgot Mandy and the skint girl and he forgot his mam's money and the lies. He even managed to get a fag from Byron. The fruit-machine, dumb television and hubbub of voices receded as they bantered over the green baize.

*

Shell left the counter, half pint in hand. Weak lager, piss-pot variety. She wished he'd carried on talking to her. They could've reminisced about school. He'd been a scrawny youth when she'd gone out with Leon, one of his mates. She was just about to mention. Perhaps he'd have resented.

No seats over by the window. As she breathed in to squeeze through the crowd in the Royal, a girl elbowed her glass. Half the contents spilled onto a young man. Over his shiny purple shirt.

'What the fuck?'

'I'm really sorry!'

The girl who'd elbowed her glass sneered at Shelly. She'd thought it an accident, now she knew it was deliberate.

The fella was with his girlfriend. If Shelly had been a bloke he'd have probably threatened her. As it was, his girl wiped the stain with a tissue, as he mumbled, 'Fuckin great!' but averted his eyes from Shelly.

She began to regret ever entering the pub. There was no room and she was stuck next to this group of girls, her feet almost off the ground. She suddenly felt a surge of aggression. Like the whole day had been building up to this point. Not even the boy's kindness could thwart it. She confronted the elbow-girl, with her permed hair sticky as candy-floss.

'What yew do tha for?'

'Oo d yew mean? I didn do nothin! Did I girlz?'

Her friends simpered and nodded.

'Fuck off! Yew knocked my glass on purpose, yew cow!'

'Well, watch oo yewr talkin to in future!'

She turned her back on Shell, as if to say, 'It's sorted!'

Shelly spun her round, clutching her bare arm and marking it. A space opened up despite the cramming, like a school fight. They wanted entertainment, clamoured for blood. A hen-pit, not cock-pit.

'I talk to oo I wan! Yew might as well ave the other arf now!'

Shelly threw the rest of her lager straight in Mandy's face. She screamed out, but Shelly didn't give her a chance to escape. Her friends backed off as Shelly swung her fist into the girl's primly made-up features and caught her chin.

There were shouts of, 'Go f'r it!' and, 'Slap er Mand!' But Mandy was reeling.

Shelly stood shaking, ready to attack again. No sooner had she made another swing for Mandy's face, than she was pulled off and dragged towards the door.

'Der! She's mad!'

'She on summin, or wha?'

Shelly struggled with the white-shirted bouncer, who flung her onto the pavement.

'Yew cun stuff yewer fuckin pub! Lager's piss anyway... Full o fuckin snobs!'

Faces at the window like faces in the classroom after being sent out. All of them goading, mocking. The muscley bouncer stood over her, defying her to do worse.

'Get ome t yewr slum!' He spat.

'Better an workin in one!'

She V-signed the faces and strode up High Street, leaving their cackling to its glass cage.

Mary regretted not having her mobile. Her dad had taken it, because she'd actually asked him to.

'I'll never get any revision done, Dad!'

'Sensible girl, that's the way. I'll do you a favour and hide it.'

She contemplated interrupting her father and that woman. What do you call it, *coitus interruptus?* It was supposed to be her dad finding her with Ant. She'd do it on behalf of her mam.

She kneeled down with ear to carpet, like listening for trains. Music played. Big band jazz. They were probably dancing, nothing more. Still, she couldn't help thinking about the poker by the hearth and an 'A' Level poem about a weapon and deceit. One of Chaucer's Tales had the same punishment in it.

Where was her mobile? He had a locked bureau in the bedroom he called his "office". As a child she'd loved to ride on his swivel-seat when he was at work. It had taken her off to shows on Barry Island and Porthcawl, the horse-roundabout or Figure of 8.

Who could she ring anyway? She had neglected all her friends when she started meeting Ant. Previously, she'd bothered with them all the time: Charl, Em, Kar and Lou. But they didn't like Ant even though Emma and Louise both came from Penybryn estate. They told her he was a "user". She just assumed they were jealous.

Now she missed them all desperately. She missed their Saturday night company at Supercool Club. All that dancing to meaningless music, losing their heads to drink and making fun of countless boys who tried to get off with them. She remembered describing one.

'Ee sayz is name's Milky. Sayz t me, "Know ow I got that name?" No, I sayz, I can't possibly guess… Ee sayz, "I'm flavour of the month down below, see. Wanna taste?" I'm allergic t milk I sayz, why don yew go shake yewr own?'

They specialized in put-downs like that. The girls were hysterical, though it never seemed as funny in retrospect.

She sat at her desk, where piles of notes were stacked in orderly fashion. Each a skyscraper she'd throw herself off. What did it mean, getting grades? It was like those films from the States: an 'A' grade pupil. Did that make her a better person?

Down below, the music stopped. She wanted her mam to haunt them, to walk out of her silver wedding photo – where he was affectionate, for the occasion – and shock them apart as they cwtched up on the sofa. Shock them forever, so they'd never defile this house again.

He was just about to start his game against Bye when the fight broke out. It was his break. As he was about to hit the white there was noise and chaos. His friends left the table to join the mêlée. He watched his cue ball clip the triangle of balls and go right down the top right pocket. He ignored the commotion, checked nobody was around and restored the white to the table in a credible position.

By the time he was bouncing up and down behind Lefty, who was basketballer height, it was all over. Some girl was being marched out the Royal. He caught glimpses of Mandy's friends flustered and fussing. He was pushed towards the window by the sheer force of bodies, in time to witness the girl from the bar badmouthing them all and doing the Penybryn wave. Sam grinned in admiration. Milky came over and began jabbering, eyes boggling with excitement.

'Sam, mun, yew'd better come over. It's Mand, she've bin jumped by some mad bitch. Mel an them reckon she wuz on summin. Jest turned on Mandy f no reason. C'mon mun!'

He'd done his hero bit already this evening and

wasn't ready to comfort a girl he felt less sympathy with than the one who'd been thrown out of the Royal in disgrace. He couldn't forget her – The girl oo didn give a fuck, he christened her. Still, he felt obliged to show an interest. Mandy's chin was cut and Mel and the others were all over her. She was swearing revenge till she saw him approaching through jammed bodies.

'What she do tha for, Mand?' he called out.

'Ow the fuck do I know? Yew wuz talking to er… She's off er bloody ead, tha's all I know… Anyway, yew'd better go n wash, yew wuz tha close to er.'

Sam didn't need a PhD in psychology to work out what had happened. Mandy's attitude said it all.

'I didn mean nothin, Mand. Jest give er some money, tha's all.'

'Give er fuckin money? Give er money? Ten minutes ago yew couldn buy us a round coz yew wuz so broke!'

He went towards her, but she pushed his shoulder away. All eyes were on their drama. He felt humiliated.

'Oh, fuck off then! She done yew real proper, didn she? If yew mus know I thought she wuz pucker!'

'Le's go girlz, I don like the smell round yer!'

She glowered at Sam and left him, friends in tow.

He couldn't concentrate on the pool after that. Milky wound him up no end. All his shots went askew.

'Givin money t gypos, eh Sam? Yew startin a fuckin charity, or wha?'

'Ne mind Oxfam,' sarked Lefty, 'it should be Ox-Sam!'

Even Bye sniggered along with them. Sam kept picturing the girl and regretted ever having given her the 5p. 'I do a good deed an then get shat on, he thought.

He was determined to retrieve the evening. It wasn't too late.

*

Shelly sat up in bed. Pillowcase colour of nicotine, a taint of being unwashed. She could still sniff gas. If she'd been a smoker she would have blown herself up before now.

She was exhilarated and ashamed at the same time. It had been worth it, hitting that ignorant bitch, but then again, what had she proved? It brought back times with her mam when she'd lashed out, attacking her mam's apathy and surrender to drugs. She couldn't work out how she hadn't been dragged down to her mam's level. Perhaps it was just that she'd learnt to stand, without ever having to crawl.

Returning to this gas-chamber, Shelly still had a sense of being watching. She had kept halting, expecting to see Clive, but hadn't caught sight of anyone. Her lock wasn't safe and the downstairs door was always open to the world and its master. She'd never been given a front door key by Castleton.

Feeling bilious, she went to the window and pushed it up. Paint flaked off, the wood soft-rotten. Below, along the road, under a streetlight, a figure moved. She was sure it was Clive, her demon, her angel or both. She surveyed her room for possible weapons. A spatula? She had one kitchen knife, but it was blunt. A crystal vase Kay had given her as a moving-in present was the most likely. She placed it next to her for comfort as she crouched by the window and drew in deep breaths of the fresh air, like inhaling tobacco-smoke. She thought she could hear Clive calling out. Was she becoming paranoid?

She peered again. When she was a kid. Spying on her mam fixing up. Going into a trance. No magic land. A country where she, Shelly, was completely forgotten. Come back, mam, come back!

The figure – it could only be Clive – was now shadow-boxing with the lamp-post! The light haloed his stumpy head and his bulbous body was awkward as he took on the object. As if he knew, he ended round one and looked in her direction. She dipped down. She crawled to her door to check the lock. It was rickety, but held fast. You could never tell. He'd seemed such a softie... and then asked her to go to that blast furnace. Her mam's friends. Some men had tickled her chin, others had terrified her with their ranting.

She went to bed, glass club beside her. In the bed-sit above, a couple were arguing. She'd said "Hiya!" to them, but little else. They had a baby and it must've woken. It was worse than white noise; their insults increased with the baby's screaming. The floorboards creaked so much, she thought they'd collapse and the whole family land on her bed in a tangle of limbs.

Sleep was a luxury she couldn't afford. She was her own bodyguard. She imagined running away from the hurt. Finding some dark place. Making her own world.

She heard footsteps up the stairs. It would be the perfect time for going to the toilet, just as they were about to open the bedroom door. She hurried out of her room and nearly collided with her dad on the landing.

He was on his own.

'Dorothy's gone home. Are you feeling sick or something?'

'No, no... jest gotta go f'r a piss, tha's all.'

She dodged around him.

'Even your language has got worse since you've known that boy.'

She left him standing there. He had to make a point

out of everything. She closed the toilet door and sat down, face in hands.

'Piss, piss, piss... I'll say it if I wanoo... it's on'y words, Dad. It's no big deal!'

Snuggled in the cosiness of her bed later, she heard the wind outside and imagined floating. It was her fantasy since she was little to have a bed that could be buoyant on the sea then lift up with the wind.

She was rock-pooling with her mam. Her mam was carefree, fishing out crabs with her bare hands and holding them up for Mary to squeal at. As ever, her mam paid no heed to her looks when she was having fun. She wore a bucket-shaped white hat and plastic bubble sandals. They were like twins many years apart. After what seemed hours of bending and netting, they returned to the crescent of sand by the steep rocks. They always chose a place like that, so her dad could position his clothes in a row, the flat rock replacing his wardrobe. He wasn't there when they got back though.

'Ee's problee gone fishin, her mam explained. But she knew her mam had made it up, because he had no interest in the sport. Still, she pursued it when he eventually turned up.

'Did yew catch anythin, Dad?'

'Catch? Only a cold I expect. It's freezing here... I've been for a walk to warm up...Don't know why we came!'

Since she could remember, he had longed to be elsewhere. Always something more important to do. Her mam gave him a withering look, but spoke affectionately to her, not to spoil her day out.

'Mary, love, we'll get yew an ice-cream later, eh? Yew'd like that, wouldn yew?'

Who needed the sun with her presence? She cwtched Mary close in a big, stripy towel.

Supercool Club super hot. Smiley face popped and Sam a true space-cadet. He was out on the dance-floor totally gone, his body twisting and turning to the shapes of the music, sweat falling like hot rain.

'Es're good!' Sam twisted to Shaman's *Ebenezer Goode*. The song like a thermal carrying him up. The girls growing feathers all ready to be plucked! They strutted and teased.

He spotted Mel, Mandy's mate, short hair and breasts practically falling out of her low-cut dress. Peacocks and peahens, but here the hens parading not the cocks.

'Wanna dance?' he lipped, ignoring the shake of her head.

'Cock-a-doodle-doo!' he crowed, from the roof of his head, 'I'm a weather-cock!'

'A total knob more like!' she yelled over the music, edging away from Sam.

The song stopped and he leaned over, catching her.

'Wan some grain? Real yard stuff.'

'Fuck off, yew dope-ead!'

She left him standing alone amongst a jam of people. The DJ announced a request and he heard it like it was force-fed down his ears through a megaphone.

'The next song's f Mandy James an er new boyfriend, Phil! They've on'y just met and are over there gettin down to it orrrready!'

Milky had managed to find Sam and was also without a partner.

'Le's do im, Sam mun!'

Milky was a crow in his black t-shirt.

'Caw, caw, caw!' Sam flew through the dancers, slicing between Anthony Pearson and Leanne Thomas. Anthony lived down the road from Sam and was a real swotty type, though you wouldn't say it to his face, because he was also sporty and half the rugby team would jump you if you insulted him.

He discovered Mandy and her new boyfriend huddled in a corner sipping cocktails with paper Union Jack flags in the glasses. He had just enough grip on reality to focus on them, though Phil was a parrot in bright green shirt, Mandy even feeding him peanuts between kisses.

'Not dancin? An this is yewr request, init?'

'The on'y dancin we do's with ower tongues, eh Phil?' she scoffed at him. 'Why don yew go find yewr gypo friend? Yew could buy a *Big Issue* off er or summin.'

He didn't recognize Phil, who was a body-builder type, showing off tan and muscles. He stared at Sam, defying him to be provocative.

'Introduce me t yewr charmin friend, Mandy.'

'Phil, this is Sam, ee's a prize dick-ead! Sam, this is Phil, ee plays rugby f Cwmtaff.'

'Warrrrk, warrrrk! Pretty polly! Get back in yewr cage!' Sam taunted the stocky, broken-beaked creature. Phil stood up and calmly pushed Sam over. He toppled backwards, stumbling down steps and breaking his fall on several couples, who moved away sensing a fight. But he was too stunned to retaliate and his wings had been clipped. Some girls had screamed out and he was a magnet for two bouncers. Seeing Phil pointing at Sam as he held Mandy, they lifted him up and hauled him off.

He felt identical to that girl. Faces laughing, all parrots pecking with remarks. Only Lefty tried to help.

'Ey, wha's goin on?' He stood in the bouncers' way, brave with the booze.

'Get out the way, less yew'd like t join yewr butty yer?'

31

From Supercool, they literally kicked him into the gutter. He sat dejected by the roadside. It was a long way down and he had travelled it too fast, like a shot had hit him mid-flight. The sharp air slapped his face. The lights of passing cars seemed to burn a thirst in him. He thought of diving in the river, drinking it in. Why couldn't it rain, so he could lie on the pavement and sup the sky?

He was grounded, would never fly again. He limped clumsily down the road. His friends wouldn't come out to see if he was alright. They'd paid too much to get in. There was nowhere else to go in Cwmtaff on a Saturday night.

The sky began to spin like a twister in the shows. Milky's flat, by the Post Office. Not far. From the bridge, the river tempted. A desert in his mouth. His tongue a cactus. He pissed in a doorway on his way to Milky's, where he'd have to wait. An elderly man and woman came out while he was doing it.

'Oh my God, Doris! Get back in, quick!'

He read the sign: Conservative Club.

'Well, they've pissed on us f long enough! Next stop, Labour Club!' he called out, running off, though his legs seemed to move slow-motion, as in a dream.

Eventually, he reached Milky's doorway and collapsed on the floor, feeling like a down-and-out. He couldn't stop the sky: no stars, no moon, just cloud-cover dark; the place where he once belonged. He shut his eyes to forget.

The ructions from above ceased for a while and Shelly drifted into a fitful sleep. She wondered if one or all of the family above were dead, and should she wake up somebody and tell them her fears. But years of hiding had made her shun involvement. Once, one of her mam's many partners in junk – might've been Brad – had flipped his lid completely. He had brandished a kitchen knife and was out to skin something. She didn't hang around long enough to find out. That was the first time she'd gone to the subway – 'ave a look, Shell. Go on! Give yew a chewing-gum or a fag!'

The subway had been dank and dreary, a home for rats, but to Shelly it was better than the risks of her house.

Half way between dream and reality, she'd pictured Clive sleeping under a lamppost, like an obedient dog. The image made him seem so innocent. She cursed her mistrust. He needed her help; he was controlled by pills.

She was woken by a key scraping in her lock. She came round quickly and grabbed the vase, tumbling out of bed as Ray Castleton, sauntered in. His eyes were glazed, his long hair unkempt.

'Yew coulda knocked!'

'Shelly girl! No need f'r the vase. Flower power, eh?' he chuckled at his own pun.

He made himself at home in the one faded armchair. She felt hemmed in. She stood by her bed as he eyed her up and down, squinting at her bare legs.

'Up early? Least, I am!' he patted his groin.

Shelly responded with aggression, the only way she knew.

'Well, Mr Castleton, what exactly d yew want?'

He crossed his legs, talking more to her thighs than her face.

'Shell, c'mon, don mess. Yew owe me, member?'

Shelly acted instinctively, like a goose at an intruder. She squeezed past him with a quiet hiss, towards the ramshackle wardrobe. He held out a hand and her knee

33

brushed it. She jerked away in disgust.

'Scuse me, Mr Castleton, but I gotta get washed n dressed.'

'Shelly! The rent!'

She took out her old flowery dressing-gown, the one Kay had lent her.

'Can yew come back arfta lunch an we cun sort it then?'

She put on a business-like tone, as if doing a deal. He leaned towards her; the gown was long and his neck was straining.

'Tell yew wha, Shell. I'll do yew a favour... I'll let yew off this month's rent.'

She knew he hadn't finished. She searched out the window. No Clive in sight. If only he could arrive now, like a strange sort of Superman.

'So where's the catch?'

'Catcha 22, Shell... Catcha 22!' for some reason he put on a phoney Italian accent.

'Eh?'

'Ne' mind... jest a film... Well, we could ave a good time, yeah?' he patted the bed.

She was beginning to panic. It was obvious he wasn't going to leave till he'd had his way. He was sitting between her and the door.

'I jest gotta go t the bogs, right?'

She acted as casually as possible, staring ahead at the door as she went past him. His hand crawled up her gown, clawing at her thigh.

She screeched out, 'Get yewr filthy mits off me!' Pulling her leg from the trap and grasping for the handle. But the trap became a human-bear, as he wound both arms round her.

'Right, Shelly! Yew wanna play it rough, yew gonna get it! It wuz gunna be makin love. Now I'm jest gonna

34

fuck yewr arse off!'

He attempted to swing her round, but she struggled, fists flying back at him. He forced her down onto the bed, mouth smothered by the soiled quilt. He was yanking up her gown and nightie, her cries muffled by the bed-clothes.

'Ge off, wanker! Yew'll go down for this!'

'I'm coming down now!' he half-laughed, half-gurgled, mouth full of spit.

She kicked out like a horse, giving it all her hatred and energy. She heard his groan. He backed off. He was doubled up, holding his balls. She was away in an instant. The front door ajar, she raced up the hill towards the estate. She had nothing left and nothing to lose.

The rare April sun dazzled into Mary's room. Today it was an intruder. A dreamless sleep. She felt cheated. Poster of Cerys Matthews in bright red outfit. She wished she had that kind of attitude. To say to *Hamlet*, Fuck yew! I got better things to do! Find Ant! Sort im out.

That was Ant's language not hers. Yet she did talk like her mam. Her dad had acquired a 'twang' – as Ant would call it – to go with all his other pretensions. The Grand Wizard, whatever they called them. Once she'd dared make fun of it – 'What d yew do with the goat, Dad? It sounds disgustin!' He had scolded her severely, telling her never to make fun of things she knew nothing about.

If only her mam had visited her dream, it would make the day possible, the sunlight bearable. Just a snatch of her in the garden singing a Welsh song like *Bugeilio'r Gwenith Gwyn*. Sad song of love and yearning.

But the day was *Hamlet* and an essay she couldn't get her head round. Her dad knocked the door.

'Mary, are you sleeping?'

What a clever question! Would she answer if she was? Still upset with him. He could've told her about this Dorothy, explained why he had to remove her mam's belongings.

'Yeah, I am. Why?'

He edged it open. He was carrying a tray full of breakfast: grapefruit, small cafetière and boiled egg in a coat her mam had knitted. A peace offering.

'Here, I thought you'd like this as a treat.'

She sat up and he laid the tray on her lap. He was hovering, seeking words in the dust motes.

'Mary!'

'Correct!'

She spooned out the grapefruit, its juice squirting into her face. Stripy jumper, smartly groomed, not a smile to be seen. Not grumpy either, just hidden.

'Thanks, Dad!' hoping he'd leave her alone.

'Mary… I want to… I mean… Didn't your boyfriend ring? Is that why you were rather rude towards Dorothy?'

She cracked the egg: beheading him.

'Yew'd be appy if we split, wouldn yew?'

'What's the point?' he turned his back on her, having the final word as he always did. 'You'll just have to get used to her. I might even marry again.'

He left. His remark aimed, arrowed.

'Yew cun stuff yewr bloody breakfast! I'm not goin to be bought!'

He was out of hearing. She shoved away the tray and the cafetière fell over, coffee spattering over her brightly-patterned duvet. She jumped out of bed and glared at her *Hamlet* text on her desk. She didn't need to write about a ghost giving instructions, she needed a ghost to guide her. She picked up her dressing-gown from the chair by the window, shading her eyes from the sun. Outside, she noticed something really weird, downhill from her house.

A girl in a nightdress and dressing-gown in bare feet dashing up the road like a fugitive from a mental hospital. It was from *Jane Eyre*. She imagined a house on fire, a tragic person imprisoned. She pressed her face to the pane. The figure was vaguely familiar, a girl her age. From school. A bunker and trouble-maker. Mary had stayed well clear of that lot.

For an instant, the girl seemed to turn her head and glance towards Mary. The expression was seething and terrified at the same time. Mary thought of opening up and calling out, asking if she needed help, but the odd girl had gone, disappearing into the sun with the rise of the road.

He came round on Milky's sofa. His mouth an empty skip, the scrapings of waste remaining. His bladder was a bag full of nails. Vague memories floated round the room: a mess of clothes, magazines and CDs. There was an empty vase with a pair of lacy knickers on top.

'Bloody weird flowers!' he thought.

Milky's annoyed voice as he held Sam over the toilet-bowl. Vomit in fountains, the worst taste in the world. Spitting out bits which stuck in his throat. Food he hadn't even eaten, layers his stomach retched up. Milky pouring water down him with some kind of funnel made from card.

His head had returned to yesterday and beat out a drumming heavier than John's band could play. A bass-drum played by a metal-fisted maniac.

He heard noises: sighing, moaning, crying out. Somebody was watching a blue movie. Probably Milky on his own, getting off on it. Sam would spring a surprise. Anyway, he was desperate for a leak.

He made his way towards Milky's bedroom. The door was shut, but the sounds were getting louder, the girl becoming very aroused.

'Ooooo... c'mon, c'mom! Tha's great! Ooah! Ooaah!'

Sam felt himself stiffen. He was reluctant now to disturb his friend's fun, but wanted a small revenge for being forgotten at the club. He edged the door open and craned his head round it.

No telly. Milky in bed. Mel on top. Didn't stop at first. Her finger in his mouth. His hands hardening her nipples. A creak. Mel heard. Halted.

'Ey, wha's up?' Milky'd moaned.

She rolled off him, covering them both with sheets.

'Fuck off Sam, will yew! Yew wanna ticket or wha?' Milky snapped at him.

'Yeah, fuck off, yew perve!' Mel echoed.

'Sorry, I thought it woz a cock film. Yew woke me up, see.'

'Don yew remember nothin? Mel woz yer las night. She elped me carry yew in when yew woz wrecked... Wise up, Sam... an piss off as soon as poss, right? Yew wuz a right pain las night an this is jest typical!'

'Yeah, great! I know where I int wanted.'

'Spoilin Mand's night an all!' Mel yelled after him.

He left them to it. He listened out, but there was nothing after that. They were probably moaning too much about him to get back to it.

Sam didn't need to be paranoid. Everything and everybody was against him. The only person who'd treated him half-decently was a girl he barely knew and might never meet again. He'd have to go home, face his mam, pay her back or lie. She wouldn't believe him. He'd done it before, cadging money for a school trip he never went on. Buying green eggs instead and drifting away up the *Res*, floating across the water without need for sails.

She ran like a girl-woman possessed up Park Avenue where the posh people lived. Every breath a relief she'd escaped being raped by that man. Every breath a feeling of disgust for letting him even touch her. Where was Clive now, her guardian angel? Running in his pyjamas out of St. Martin's and into town? The image made her think how they had more in common than she'd thought.   She dodged around an elderly couple on their way to church. The man caught hold of his wife's arm like Shelly was a mad axe-woman!

For a second, she averted her eyes from straight-ahead vision. In an upstairs window she saw a girl her age she thought she recognized from school. She was so smug and comfortable in that huge house with its drive. She was peering down with such condescension.

Every breath she exhaled loathing for Ray Gun – the bastard pig! Shit-eater! Weasel wanker! She couldn't think of enough insults to suit him. Kay had said she should work for a paper, she had a way with words.

Kay. That was it. She realized where she was going. She couldn't move back, but at least Kay could help. She ran into Penybryn estate. A man in his boxers taking in the milk shouted over –

'Ey, love, yew look as if yew need a bed! I got a spare one!'

She ignored him and ran on. The houses so well-kept here, but further on the newer part told of poverty and neglect. Towards the Community Centre a stray mongrel leapt out after her. It snapped at her bare feet, seeing meat. She swiped and it barked viciously, just missing one of her fingers with its sharp fangs. It bounded after her, till she took off the belt of her gown as bait. It fell for the ploy and tore at it, like Rottweiler with rabbit.

Round the corner from the shops, her old house, 23 Snowdon. Her close was a tip! She stopped dead. An empty space! A line of rubble where the row of houses used to be. Some of Snowdon stood, but a whole terrace had been demolished. Most had been boarded up the last time she saw it, yet she was still stunned. Opposite, were two blocks of flats: one lived in and the other with most windows boarded up. They used wood now, cheaper than metal. Showed they'd soon follow.

She had nowhere to go while houses were being knocked down. But she was glad to see number 23 reduced to shattered stone. She trod carefully over the line, straining to trace the place where it had stood. A boy on a bike did a wheelie, than accelerated towards her down the path. He had a cheeky face and troublesome hair.

'Lookin f summin?'

'Yeah, my ol ouse.'

He eyed her suspiciously.

'Yew bin kicked out?'

'Sort of.'

'Yew wanna get yewrself one o them flats. Mind they'll be knockin them down soon, as well.'

'Wha's yewr name?'

'Marc with a 'c'. Arfta Marc Bolan. It's the Welsh spellin. Marc Bolan wuz a rock star ages ago, y know.'

'Are yew my guardian angel, Marc?'

Shelly held out her hand, as though for him to kiss.

'Razory stitch!'

'Shouldn ewse bard language at yewr age.'

'It's not. It's summin I learnt.'

Shelly gazed at the flats and an idea came into her head. A crazy notion, but what else? She'd see Kay first though. Kay would make her believe again.

Marc reared his bike like a bucking bronco, then gobbed on the path.

'Anyway, I'm in the Comp now!'

'I ewsed t go there too. I woz ewsually bunkin off though.'

His eyes widened with admiration.

'Where d yew go?'

'Dunno... anywhere... downtown... Cardiff... whatever.'

Marc became bored and rode over the rubble jerking his head. 'What they call yew anyway?'

'Shelly.'

'Arfta oo?'

Shelly shivered and began walking towards the home, rubbing her hands furiously.

'Some poet bloke, I think.'

'Hairy-O clink!' Marc rhymed, then cycled off.

Oo's madder, that kid or me? thought Shelly.

The flats would be easy, but it would be short-term. On one of their walls was scrawled graffiti 'DONNA LUVS LEE'. On another the burn-marks of a fire. The one thing she could do at school. Never really had a chance. Walls should entertain, enlighten, demand, Look at me!

The sun soon got drowned in cloud, as Mary lifted a biro and nibbled at it. The mirror gave no clues what she should do. Polonius's ghost wanted to fix her to her desk all day analysing, quoting, dissecting the play

41

till it was left in tatters. She sat down to make a plan. Ended up scribbling – *Ant Where?   What happened?*

Dear Ant,
    You mustn't ever do that again. I worry so much. I am Ophelia. I am insane with love.

She chewed her biro, then slammed it down hard. What was the point? If nobody told her, she'd have to tell herself. But it was a voice, like her mam's, which spoke from inside – Mary, dress up tidy. Go an see im. Sort it out once an fr all.

She obeyed her mam's instructions, putting on a cream blouse and black skirt which resembled church-wear. Then a felt jacket, so as not to overdo it. Told her dad she was going to Lisa's to discuss her essay. He fell for it, delighted she'd come round to her sensible self.

Her thoughts wavered to and fro. She followed the path of that strange girl, up hill towards Penybryn. No buses on Sunday, of course. The streets deserted. Sunday dead-day, hangover day, recovery day. Sun long gone.

Ant's house wasn't too far, Penyfan Road. Sounded picturesque, but just a long line of houses each one like the next. Ant must've gone to the hospital with his invalid father. He'd done so before when he hadn't turned up downtown for a shopping trip. He was always saying how sick his dad was.

A youth walked towards her, carrying a guitar. He slouched and his hair was bedraggled. She had an idea he used to go to her school. He grinned as they passed.

She felt alien, smart clothes incongruous even on the Sabbath.

She needed to see him urgently. 76 Penyfan. She counted the numbers. It was like lift-off. She'd wanted to visit before, but he had insisted, not ashamed but too preoccupied with his father's disability.

Number 76 was fenced and had a porch extension. It even had a burglar alarm. There was a cloying smell of fresh paint. She knocked the brass knocker and squinted into the peep-hole. After a while, the white UPVC door spoke: 'If yewr a Jovy's Witness, we're not intrested! We're defnitlee CofE. yer.'

At first she was flummoxed. Then she looked up as a window opened above and a plump woman leaned out.

'Um... Mrs Pearson... I've come to see Anthony. I'm Mary...Tell im I'm yer please. Ee wuz sposed t phone las night!'

'Oh my God! I'll be down right now, love!'

The shock on her face worried Mary. Pictures of accidents flashed through her mind. Ant under a lorry. Ant lying, broken up, on the pavement.

Mrs Pearson soon came to the door, ushered her in and asked her to sit down. There was no sign of a wheelchair.

'Cuppa tea, Mary?'

'Yes please. Is Anthony orright, Mrs Pearson?'

'Yeah... far as I know, that is.'

Ant's mam disappeared into the kitchen. The house was less immaculate on the inside. Ant's old trainers deposited on the carpet and a pizza box sitting in one armchair. Signs of the son, but not the father.

'Ow d yew mean? Where is ee?' Mary asked, when she returned. She couldn't stop anxiously shifting and chewing the flesh round her nails.

'Ee's not in, love. Ee didn sleep yer las night. Slept

over is fren's.'

'Which friend?'

Mrs Pearson handed her the cup and offered her a biscuit. Mary declined. Mrs Pearson sat down next to her on the sofa. She kept staring at Mary in pity. On the mantelpiece was a photo of her, slimmer and vibrant with her husband. He reminded Mary of Ant, stocky and large-eyed, with that teasing smile which had attracted her so much.

'Is yewr usband bard?'

'My usband?' Mrs Pearson was aghast.

'Yeah?'

'Ee died, five years ago. Eart attack. Didn Ant say?'

'No!' Mary's eyes sank into the cup. 'My mam too... she died...of cancer...I miss er terrible.'

Mrs Pearson sank back into the sofa, immersed in memories. Mary brought her back.

'I'm sorry, Mrs Pearson, but which fren did yew say ee woz with? I need t see im desperately.'

Mrs Pearson began to speak, but didn't seem to be addressing Mary. She was scolding her son, even in his absence.

'Didn oughta ave treated yew like this. It int fair, I gotta say it. Lovely girl like yew an all.'

Mary stood abruptly in front of her, so she had to speak directly.

'Mrs Pearson... where is ee... Please?'

She averted her eyes towards the mantelpiece and the photo Mary had observed.

'Please?' Mary knelt, in prayer-position.

Mrs Pearson sighed, 'Ow long yew bin meetin im, Mary?'

'Three months, at least. Why?'

She sighed again, touching Mary lightly on the arm. Mary wanted to hug her, to prevent her from telling.

Yet, she also wanted to know.

'Yew'd better know, dear... my own son. I'm ever s
sorry. Ee stayed over with is girlfren Leanne... I mean
is other... Ee's a two-timin sod, Mary. Ee've treated
yew...'

She didn't let her finish. Tears shook her body as she
ran from the house. He had taken her feelings and
knifed them. She held onto the wall outside. Tears
clogged her throat. She didn't want to swallow for
breath. She wanted the tears to keep bleeding from her
till she dried up. She heard Ant's mam – 'Mary! Come
back inside, le's talk!'

But she couldn't face her. She staggered up the road,
unaware of the direction. All that desire, that love he
had murdered. In mourning for herself.

He escaped before Milky and Mel woke up. He took
the white floral knickers as a souvenir. He felt they
might cheer him up. At least his body felt better,
purged of its poisons.

He was going home because he had nowhere else to
go. He hoped they'd all be out, so he could collapse on
his bed and sleep off a weird night. Just as he thought
things were fine, his head started to play up, a
demolition ball swinging against his skull-walls. If he
could graffiti them now it would say, Balls to the
World. The weather matched his mood. It started to
rain as he left High Street for the hill climb.

Rounding the corner, a man approached him. He
recognized him, though didn't know him personally.
The ponytail and hippy gear marked him out. It was
Ray Gun. Sam knew boys who worked for him. Girls
too. It was too late to avoid him. Ray was agitated, eyes
twitchy.

'Ey son! Seen this girl? Looks dead scruffy… wearin a dressin-gown. She've done a runner with my bread, see.'

At first, Sam thought of a stolen loaf. Then it clicked. One of his girls on the run. Probably beaten up by a client. Worse, by Ray Gun's cronies. But close up, Castleton wasn't any threat. Despite the dragon tattoos on his arms, he had a pleasant expression once he calmed down. Sam knew from school the best policy was to join the bullies. He was also gasping for a fag, having cadged only a few the night before and now broke.

'I could look out f'r er…let yew know like.'

'Castleton knew that hungry expression; it was the blood he drank.

'Yeah, nice one, man… Tell yew wha, yer's my card. Any info on er, let me know straight away, right? There'll be a reward, o course.'

Sam took the professionally-printed business card: CASTLETON PROPERTIES. He wondered if he'd been wrong about this man. Perhaps he'd been a victim of jealousy and rumour. Plenty in Cwmtaff had been condemned by these.

'Mr Castleton… it's no problem… uh… yew aven got a fag t spare by any chance?'

'A fag? Don be fuckin stewpid, yer, ave the rest of this packet! An don forget, yew come 'cross tha bitch, ring my mobile. She's off er fuckin ead, so don mess with er. Right? Wonky front teeth. Bout 19… Nice t do business with yew… er?'

'Sam.'

'Tidee, Sam. Sam the Man, eh?'

Ray Gun slapped Sam's shoulder. Gold rings on each finger like an ornate knuckle-duster. Sam felt proud. He had a sense of purpose for once. He took a fag out and Castleton actually lit it for him.

'S long, Mr Castleton. Ta f the fags!'

'S long, Sam. Ey, keep in touch anyroad. I might ave some work f yew.'

'Great stuff! I will, aye!'

The uphill slog didn't tire him and even rain freshened him now. On Ray Gun's side nobody could get you. He could tell his mam he'd got work. His dad couldn't care less, spending his time semi-conscious down the club since he'd lost his job.

Castleton had noticed a pair of knickers dangling from Sam's back pocket. Boy arfta my own eart, he thought. Sam had forgotten about them. In one front pocket a packet of fags, in the other a business card. He felt he could seize the sky and tear a hole in it for the sun to poke through.

'Whappnin little brawd! Yew look in a right state!' It was like hitting a lamppost. John was opposite, guitar slung over his shoulder.

'Yew gotta fuckin cheek I mus say!'

The rain made John even more scarecrow-like, as he crossed the road looking smug.

'Mam's gonna fuckin murder yew. Fi wuz yew, I'd go inta idin. What bout yewr mucker Milky? Carn yew stay with im till she cools it?'

'I'll fuckin pay er back. Coupla days, no prob.'

'Ow, yew bin dealin or summin?'

'Gotta job!'

'Yeah, an I got an album deal with Richard Branson. Wise up, kid!'

'Fuck off!' Sam spat and carried on towards their house.

'Yeah, an good mornin t yew good sir... Fuckin loser!'

Sam knew a short-cut through the subway. Most of

the subways had been filled by the Council. Too much litter, too many lager-drinkers and glue-sniffers. As if the subways were to blame.

So what if he did find this prozzie? What was she to him, except a 'reward', as Castleton put it? Maybe she had stolen from him. She deserved to be punished for it. Sam had been cheated by women too often: Mand with her new boyfriend and Mel riding Milky all night, while he slept in his own spew. They had to be taught.

He passed a house in Penyfan Rd, some girl sniffling by the porch. It was pathetic! How could she show her weakness like that? He sneered. From now on he would not be used, like an item of clothing, to be worn then discarded when the time suited.

Kay in Porthcawl on the shows. Zooming down the log-flume, embracing Shelly as her mam had never done. Shrieking delight as water sprayed them.

Kay in Abersarn, on one of those ridiculous outward bound courses Shelly loathed. Even she could make it a laugh. Making a raft from old wooden crates. Kay using a branch to punt! Getting it stuck in the mud, hanging on as the raft carried on downstream. Left dangling like a puppet with cut strings. Face like a moon. Not the moon, but another one, a reddish moon which always glowed for Shelly on those nights when she'd given up. Her moon. And even when the wrong colour, the moon always recalled Kay. During lonely times since she had to leave Dan-y-graig, she would stare at it, willing it to be that face.

She felt a failure going back. She'd wanted to return in glory, like a Hollywood star, to make Kay proud. Now here she was, crawling, a creature stripped of everything but her night-clothes.

Approaching the entrance, she prepared her story. The last thing she needed was the police. Every plot she concocted seemed too incredible though. A fire? Not in a dressing-gown this far away. Clothes stolen by a burglar during the night? Kay would guess anyway. She'd tell her the truth, but less dramatic. He just attempted to fondle her. She'd hit him and, panicking, escaped.

She pressed the buzzer and a voice came through the small mike. It was familiar. It was Jan, one of the care workers. She'd hated Shelly, blamed her for most of the trouble.

'Yes, who is it?'

'It's Shelly Bush... Cun I speak to Kay... I mean, Mrs Davies, please?'

'She's not yer anymore. What do yew want?'

'Please! I need t see er. It's really important!'

'She isn't yer, but I'll come down down, orright?'

Eventually, Jan opened the reinforced door and eyed Shelly harshly, arrowed features targeting.

'Der, yew do look in a right state, Shelly. What ave yew been up to now?'

Shelly returned her pointed expression.

'I aven bin up to anythin... I mus see Kay...I need t talk about summin.'

Jan smiled in a malicious way, enjoying Shelly's situation.

'She's gone. Moved to another post. Got promotion!'

'Crap!'

Shelly shoved her aside and darted into Dan-y-graig Home. A girl she knew, Donna, was sitting on the stairs. Her eyes popped as she witnessed Shelly kicking the door to Kay's old office. A human typhoon in a dressing-gown! Jan pursued her.

'Ey, Shelly! Stop! What yew doin?'

She knew from the room's prim neatness Kay had gone. She thrust her face into Donna's, spitting her questions –

'Where is she? Kay? Mrs Davies? Where?'

Donna shook with the impact of Shelly's anger.

'I dunno! Onest.'

Jan caught up and grabbed her by the arm. She threw it off like a dog had sunk its teeth in.

'Shelly, yew don want to get arrested f trespassin now, do yew? Just come into my office an we'll chat about this.'

Shelly was breathing heavily, eyes jittering from wall to wall.

'Bollocks! Jest give me some tidee clothes an I'll bugger off, right?'

But Jan had to have control, so she tried to put her hand on Shelly's arm again, this time a dog sniffing.

'Shelly, I'm sure we can elp if yewll just calm down.'

'Fuck it! I don need no charity. I cun sort myself out!'

Shelly burst out of the home, crashing the door like a coffin-lid. As far as she was concerned, her past was dead. If it wasn't for that seed of a plan, the present and future could join it. She escaped to the place of refuge she'd always sought. Down the road was the dark subway where she had buried all thoughts of her mam and now Kay would be the same. The moon would no longer bring her hope.

She lost her sense of direction. Her stinging, bloodshot eyes had blurred everything. Only realized where she was when she saw graffiti on a wall opposite the shops, telling her where to go –

LEANNE + ANT

Join her mam. Communicate, even if it wasn't talk. Her father was right. She hadn't listened. Like a simple answer, a single shop was open, the Spar. Sold them in small numbers now. Buy one packet, slip the rest down her blouse. A bottle of water to wash them down. Simple and direct. Soon mam. Soon Ant would regret it. Cheating her. Treating her like an item to be opened, used and not even re-cycled. Soon he'd suffer. She must convince. Put on an act. Her dad would listen at last. Her mam would welcome.

Mary brushed her hair, wiped her face with a tissue. Straightened up and gulped back her desire to sob. Show them what.

The Asian man at the counter was reading his paper, ignoring her. She was still terrified. She'd shake and all the packets would scatter! When she found them she couldn't decide which to buy and steal. Capsule? Tablet? Dissolvable? She'd never stolen before. At least she looked respectable. She scanned the shop. He was indifferent. Whipped four packets under her blouse, loosened ready. She picked one to buy, tucking herself in.

At the counter, she tried to seem confident. Gave a weak smile as she passed the water and Paracetemol.

'I've got a bit of n angover!'

'Yes, I can see that.'

He answered mechanically. Wasn't concerned. She felt triumph leaving the shop. She hoped the camera had recorded her and that her father and Ant would get to see it. A girl who knew her destiny.

The shops: dingy, rundown. Where pupils who couldn't care less went lunchtimes from her school. Out of bounds.

Not any longer.

Round the back it was deserted. No-one to interfere.

51

She slumped against a wall. The rain had stopped, but gloom prevailed. The damp ground soaked her skirt. She lay among discarded cans and takeaway cartons.

From inside her, her mam's voice implored once again –

'I miss yew, Mary! I miss all them talks we ad.'

She popped a pill in her mouth and took a swig. Every pain would go away but it would take time. One for her father, one for Ant, one for that girl who'd stolen him, one for her mam's dying and the person she became, shrunk to a rotten stump. One for the friends she dropped, one by one. One for the pointless work, desk piled with words but not an answer in sight.

She was inside the wardrobe. The door was locked, but she didn't struggle in hide-n-seek. She was immersed in her mam's clothes and shoes. The vaguely perfumed, but musty odour of them making her feel sleepy yet sick. They fell on top of her, one after the other: jumpers, dresses, skirts, blouses. There were drifts of clothes smothering her. She never once fought for air. This was where she belonged, what she wanted most.

The rain stopped in sympathy with his buoyant mood. He was ready to take on his mam, promise her payback with knobs on!

'Mam, I gotta job in property!' it sounded very important, but she wouldn't be that gullible.

'Mam, I got work as a rent collector. It's pucker pay!' That was more credible. 'I woz desperate for the twenty t meet somebody. Ad t buy im a few pints. Give me the job arfta.'

He'd grovel like that. It would be worth it. Even being grounded would do his head a lot of favours.

The subway took him under Everest Ave. As he descended the slope, suitable for wheelchairs, pushchairs, skateboards and rollerblades, the stench of piss gave him a swift uppercut. In the absence of public lavs, Cwmtaff had provided bus-shelters and subways. He hated places like this, preferring the mountains and magies: the thrill of dancing with trees while his friends' heads turned into balloons! In drab autumn, it was like living a cartoon.

So he walked straight past a crouched bundle of rags on the ground, till it stirred and he jumped in shock. A girl's face peeked up at him, damp and shivering.

'Yew orright?'

He cautiously approached her, stooping. It was the crazy girl from the Royal! Her eyes even harder, two screwdrivers. She was wearing a smutty dressing-gown and a patterned nightie stuck out from under it. He didn't want to ask her too many questions, in case it was upsetting and she'd start blaring. He couldn't handle that right now.

'Fuckin ell, it's Miss Frank Tyson erself! Wha's appened? Yew wuz fuckin famous las night, yew know. Evryone wuz talkin.'

Shelly was glad to see him. He'd helped her last night and even if he failed to intervene later, she still felt he cared. She stood up, hugging herself for warmth.

'Yew come t save me agen, ave yew?'

'I don know 'bout that! Ey, tell yew wha, yew got real style. I loved the way yew sorted Mandy an give em all the Pen wave...Wha's yewr name, by the way, I never remembered?'

'Shelly. Wha's yewers?'

'Sam. Sam Taylor. They called me "Toilet" in school. I carn think why.'

'Toilet, eh? Yewr in-a right place then!'

53

Shelly grinned and exposed her lopsided teeth. It hit Sam like a jab to his chin. This was the runaway. She was the reward!

'Wha's up with yew. I didn mean nothin by it. On'y a joke!'

'No, no… it's nothin… bard memrees, tha's all.'

Conflicting thoughts fought in his head. To ring Castleton, get the money. To befriend her. He couldn't decide. He'd wait, work it out.

Shelly took the lead.

'Le's get outta yer. I'm beginnin t feel like a rat!'

'Aye, yew look a bit like one an all.'

'Cheeky bugger!'

Ahead, she spotted something draped out of his back pocket. A pair of fancy white knickers of all things!

'So ow come yewr in night stuff then? Get kicked out or summin?'

Shelly avoided answering. The rain had begun again. Her stomach was as empty as the flats opposite.

'Where d yew get them knickers from, yew a perve or wha?'

Sam took them from his pocket.

'Na, I nicked em. Nicked! Ge it? They're a souvenir! Tell yew wha…'

They walked on. Shelly wasn't sure where they were heading.

'…ave yew got any on?'

'Think I'd tell yew?'

'Anyway, ave these. Yew need em more n me I reckon.'

'They clean?'

'Yeah, not too many skid-marks!'

Sam examined them, sniffing. Shelly took them and laughed. It was an odd laugh. A laugh to shoot you down. She slipped off her pocked moccasins and put on the knickers. She couldn't afford to be choosy. She had a memory-flash of a beach and Kay making fun of her modesty in a friendly way.

'Shelly, it's not as if yew've got anythin to ide, is it?'

Sam didn't return to the topic of her situation and she was relieved by what she perceived as tact. They were heading for the shops.

'By the way, where're we goin?' she asked.

'I wuz gunna ask yew the same question.'

She paused, sizing him up: spiky hair down to trainers splattered with dubious stains.

'Well, all I need is food, clothes an a roof over my ead... any ideas?'

'Wanna fag?' he offered Shelly a cigarette, 'trouble is, I got no light.'

The rain dribbled down her face. There was little left of last night's fighter, even her eyes pleaded now.

'Tell yew wha, come t my ouse. I'm in real shit...nicked money off of my mam. Seein yew ull elp. I'll tell er yewr my new charity. She might go soft.'

'So, Sam Taylor, the money yew give me wasn even yewr own. Tha's why yew woz so generous!'

She loathed the idea of charity and didn't know if he could be trusted, but it was her only chance.

Penybryn shops were shuttered up except for the Spar. Graffiti was scrawled over most of the roller-blinds, from names, initials and tags to –

Fuck the law

Just take draw.

Shelly wanted to pattern them with weird shapes, spiders' webs in space. Their boring grey deserved to be graffitied, though it was the visual equivalent of gobbing. One stood out as they neared the Spar. It was the tag Carboy and an effort at real graffiti art, with bubble-writing and bright spray. Carboy was, at least, starting to know his territory. Her stomach rumbled like an express train. Sam heard it because he was so attentive, keeping a close watch all the time.

'Tell yew wha, shull I ge some munchies in-a Spar?'

He searched his pockets. Took out the business card. Couldn't believe his stupidity.

'What's tha?'

'Oh, nothin… jest a contact… I forget, I blew it all las night.'

They stood in front of the small store. The smell of a Sunday roast from the flats above made Shelly's belly growl discontent. Sam was still too hung over to want to eat much.

'Yew wouldn?'

'Oh, yeah, I did ave one frog coin, o course.'

Sam glanced through the shop-window.

'No prob! I'll sort it!'

A couple of minutes later, he came out with a Mars bar, which he offered to Shelly.

'Yewr breakfast, ma'am.'

They continued towards the gap by the betting-office, another short-cut to Sam's.

'Yew skanked it!'

'Scuse me, I did not! I'm jest a Paki-lover, tha's all. I speak the language.'

He accented the last sentence in stage Asian. When Shell didn't respond, he was annoyed.

'Wha's up, don yew believe me?'

'Na, it isn tha… it's jest… I carn stan ignorance!'

'Oh ho… lissen t Miss Righteous, eh? Well, oo sayz 'frog' an not 'French' then?'

Suddenly, he stopped dead. Shell followed his stare. On the ground, slumped against the wall was the body of a girl, smartly dressed. Their eyes exchanged panic signals. Both were on the verge of flight, thinking it was a corpse left in the secluded and dark alley, surrounded by high walls. Then Shell saw the packets near the body.

'Sam, look! Pills! We better get er up the ospital quick!'

'Shit! I don need this! Carn we jest phone then leg it?'

'I don bleeve yew.' Shelly took charge. 'Yew elped me. Wha's the fuckin difference, Sam?'

Sam thought he had enough on his hands with Castleton's girl. Then he recognized the girl on the ground.

'Fuckin ell, I seen er earlier. She woz blarin outside this ouse down-a road. Didn she ewsed t go up-a Comp.?'

Shelly also felt the face was familiar. But she was too busy to dwell on it.

'Orright, I'll stay with er an yew phone n ambulance.'

The torn up pill packets were deposited round the girl. She was drained of colour, but her hand still felt warm. Shell knew enough to move her onto her side. She was a looker with high forehead and wavy hair. Shelly couldn't recall her name from school, but she was bright, a real swot and must still be in the sixth form. Shelly held her palm, kneading it like it was dough and would rise.

'Bloody ell, gul, what bastard's made yew do this, eh?'

Shell was back in time, standing over her mam, who was comatose on the floor. White powder, needles, tablets: the only food and drink her mam's hunger and thirst craved. She was spread out, dead to Shell's calls – 'Mam, mam! Wake up! Please, mam! Wake up!'

She started, as Sam came back, voice jabbering.

'Right, le's fuck off Shelly. I phoned the ambulance. Give em a location an all.'

'We carn leave y dopey sod!'

'Oh yeah? Say the cops come, see yew in yewr nightgear. They're gunna ask questions, in ey?'

Sam approached the collapsed girl and all the time Shelly was whispering to her, a quiet chant, desperate not to lose her completely. Sam leant over.

'Fuckin ell, I member er now! Mary summin, er dad's a Councillor... She woz a real swot...Wha's she doin up yer? Shelly, this is getting worser...We gotta go quick!'

As he finished, they heard the siren. The hospital was less than a mile on the other side of the estate. Sam caught hold of Shell's sleeve and she swept it away in annoyance.

'Lissen, Sam, some twat's done this to er. I carn leave er! Yew go if yew wan!'

Sam's focus switched from Mary, smart skirt and velvet jacket stained by alley dirt, to Shelly, who looked like an angry sleep-walker. He couldn't help admiring Shelly's tenacity. He was her only hope, yet she clung to this girl as if she were a lost friend. Then he recalled Castleton and the bounty on her body.

'Orright, I'll stay, but why don yew change clothes with er? Yew need em more than er!'

'Wise up, Sam. Don talk darft!'

Shell's hair was straggly and wild and as she bent over the lying girl, still reassuring, Sam imagined the curve of her slim body underneath the night-clothes. He thought of those white knickers hugging the V. He couldn't. He couldn't possibly fancy this state of a girl like something out of *Oliver!*

The siren got louder. 'Gotta go! Gotta go! Gotta go!'

'Mary, Mary! Don worry... It won' be long now!'

'She carn yer yew. She's out of it!'

When the ambulance arrived, the two men got out

and rapidly assessed the situation. As one began giving oxygen to Mary, the other collected up all the packets and carefully bagged them. All the time, he was asking them questions and Sam had the cheek to ask him for a light! Shell couldn't believe how insensitive he could be.

'Ow come yew aren't dressed?' the burlier man questioned Shelly.

'I live over the shops. I seen er from my window, so I come down straight away.'

The other was attempting to get some response from Mary, but to no avail. When they'd parcelled her up and began carrying her into the ambulance, Shell enquired, 'Can I come with er, please?'

Sam glared at her. What was she playing at?

'No, I don think so, love. It's not as if yewr a relative, is it?'

But even as they were getting into the vehicle, Shell didn't give up.

'Sam... my boyfren yer... ee'll run an get some clothes f me... Oh please!'

Without getting an answer, she'd scrambled into the back and they weren't going to evict her.

Sam was taken aback to be called her boyfriend, but he didn't like it. He was supposed to be in control of her and didn't want to be separated, but could hardly hop in after her. He decided to run as fast as he could to the hospital and find them there. As the driver sped off, alarms blaring and lights flashing, Sam swore and headed for the first of many short-cuts he knew through the estate.

Shell knew what would happen to Mary. Her stomach would be pumped. If they could get her there fast enough that is. Her face was a white mask. Shell knew about the pump, because one of her mam's friends had OD'd and not even that could save her. This friend, Brenda, had been special to Shelly. She had always brought her treats and she looked after her when her mam was incapable. Brenda wanted a kid and couldn't have one, her mam told her in a lucid moment. At the funeral, Shell made a vow to the soil never to go like that.

Out of the back window of the ambulance, she glimpsed the flats she'd seen earlier. The sky was dour and grey above them. If only you could paint the sky itself: a rainbow, the northern lights.

A hand tugging at her through the gap in the cupboard door. Her mam's, yet she saw no face. She made efforts to cry out, but could only lip the words ineffectually, 'Mam, I'm coming! I'll be there!'

She was bound and embalmed in her mother's clothes now. The imitation fur coat she hated so much made up the final layer. They didn't comfort any more, rather they pressed tight constricting her ribs. There was a nylon film across her mouth the texture of tights. Whenever she sucked in to breathe, it masked her mouth.

It was a journey: the sea after all. She was cargo. She wanted out of this cupboard-coffin. Her arms and legs limp and useless, she let her body fall against the door like a trust game; but who would catch her?

She tumbled out and instead of sea, she fell and fell through the sky till she hit the surface and her body was transformed. It became seal-like: breathing out of pores in her skin. The water her home now, with clothes shed like snake-skin. Her last visions were of coats and dresses bubbling upwards, cloth-fishes drawn by the hooks of hangers.

Then there was nothing but the sea. She breathed liquidly, could hear a distant engine, like a boat above in another world.

As Mary was taken from A&E to the high dependency area, Shelly was told by one of the porters to get back to her ward.

Sam joined her, puffing and panting like a miniature steam engine. He seemed genuinely pleased to see her and even pecked her cheek like a true boyfriend anxious about his sick girl.

Shelly watched Mary being wheeled away, disappearing like a train down a tunnel. She knew that she couldn't abandon her. She felt they had something in common, despite their backgrounds. That sad, pale face haunted her, as if she had witnessed it somewhere else, maybe in a dream. Mary's clothes might fit, but it wasn't the clothes that kept her there.

Sam, however, seemed anxious for escape. He was thinking about getting Shelly up his house long enough for 'Ray Gun' to pick her up. She was the cash and problems solved

'Orright! We off then?'

Again she was angered by his impatience.

'No way I'm leavin er!'

'What's it t yew? Er dad'll sort evrythin if she comes round. F fuck's sake, yew comin or wha?'

A passing nurse overheard Sam and narrow-eyed suspicion.

'Excuse me, visitin's over! Which ward yew on, love?'

Sam raised his eyes in exasperation. 'Right, I'm off!'

He expected Shelly to follow, a stray dog in need of food and shelter.

'I'm on Natal!'

The nurse X-rayed Shelly's gown with bespectacled eyes.

'I… ad a miscarriage, see. My boyfren yer reckons I'm fit t leave, but I don feel right yet… S long, Sam… see yew tomorrow!'

Shelly could lie on her feet. The Homes had taught her that. Even Kay had fallen for it one night when she got back late, after sex in a stolen car with Leon. An elaborate story about visiting Brenda's grave up on the hillside and no buses back.

The nurse seemed satisfied, as the young man shuffled away and the very smutty young girl went towards the lift.

Sam played along with her drama, though he wasn't sure what she was up to. He wouldn't let her go that easily. He gripped Castleton's business card in his pocket till it hurt. "My boyfren yer". She said that so convincingly, but it was an act.

Shell scurried into the lift like a very smeary White Rabbit. She'd loved *Alice* as a kid. Her mam had played a song about it, by some group called *Jeff's Aeroplane* or such like. Her favourite present was the gloriously illustrated book. She cartooned herself once as Alice, but instead her mam had taken the medicine. It's all in the head, the White Rabbit said.

Natal. She'd been there before. One of her mam's friends had given birth to a lovely boy, Gavin. Born an addict. Had to be weaned off from birth.

Sam left behind. Was he a pimp or dealer, or was he different? She wasn't sure, but Mary was her hope now. The flat idea grew. Her father a Councillor as well. It seemed to be taking shape.

Little Gavin craving heroin not milk. White lies.

White Rabbit leading you down. Too big for the house, her head needing to reach the sky.

She hung round the waiting-room door, knowing that the nurses were too rushed to pay her attention. She only needed enough time for Mary to live or die. Shell had a feeling she'd recover though, there had been the hint of a grip, like tiny Gavin holding onto her index finger.

They had fished her out. Here she was lying on the bank, the sky a white ceiling. Mary lay, her stomach an open wound. They had hooked into her mouth and reached down into her guts, yanking at them till her body surfaced.

'Mam, I'm sorry I never made it!'

The uniformed fisher-nurse comforted.

'Alright, love, don't fret!'

Line remained attached to her arm. She wanted to pull it out. To free herself.

'Now, now! That's enough!'

She was restrained. An infant again, too near heat. Through wavy eyes she made out a screen, graph movements jerking with her heart; observed its rise and fall with amazement; a small landscape of valleys and hills, her geography and now, her life.

She knew she'd have to grow legs again. The fisher-nurse would help her. Once a mermaid in another world and now a girl washed up. She shut her eyes and imagined collecting her mam's belongings all along the tide line, beachcombing for memories.

'What's yewr name, love, yewr name?'

'Ask my dad, he might remember!'

'Okay, love. I'll leave yew be f now. Ave a little sleep, it'll do yew good.'

She was a failure, but she'd come through. She was someone else, but she wasn't certain yet who that was. Her stomach hollow as though she had given birth to something, but it had been born dead. Her past. No way to swim back in. She floated in her bed waiting for a wind that would rise and take her over the hills and valleys, the tracings of her heart-beat.

Sam hung around the entrance, wondering whether to abandon Shelly totally. He could phone Castleton's mobile straight away, but there was no guarantee she'd stay put. A huddle of pregnant women were smoking on the other side of the doorway. Sam saw his opportunity as one threw away her stub. He approached casually, taking out his packet.

'Wan one, love?'

'Der, thanks! I shouldn, mind. An yew shouldn be temptin me neither!'

'Sorright, my missis is in Natal. Jest in t day. Ad a miscarriage…'

'Sorry, love!'

'I need t see er, but visitin's over. I need t tell er summin important.'

The woman was probably twenty odd, but her face was in the forties, gaunt structure and dusty skin. The other two ignored him as she took a fag and lit it.

'Tell yew wha, I'll pass on yewr message. Wha's er name?'

Sam was tripped and stumbled a second.

'Same as mine. Taylor. Shelly Taylor… Thanks, love… Tell er I'll wait f'r er b yer… Tell er Sam's er man!'

'Eh? Yew shewer yewr married. Sounds a bit too romantic t me!'

*

Shell felt simultaneously awkward and at home amongst all the hill-bellied girls and women. Her stomach a level plain. Her night-clothes at last fitting in. She'd lost her baby, Mary. But she'd find her again: another Mary, who she'd take away. She wanted to explain the story to everyone, how she would have had a little girl.

She sat in the TV lounge, hoping the food trolley would come soon, even if it was soggy chips and yoghurt the texture of superglue. She sensed their eyes on her mid-riff, making small holes like fag-burns. She couldn't just launch into the tale of her miscarriage. On TV, couples confessed their sins:

'I'll never go back to him. Never! He put sex before everything, killed our child before it was born. I was pregnant, see, and he was always insisting…'

She didn't know if it was their story or hers she was hearing.

A woman entered, wheezing like a miner with 'the dust'. She took her time to speak, looking round the room.

'Anyone called Shelly Taylor yer?'

Shell started at the first name. Checked to see if anyone else responded. Remembered Sam's surname, as the woman focussed on her, the only stranger.

'Yew Shelly Taylor or wha?' The skinny woman supported her bulge with both hands, propping it up. She saw Shelly's lack of a bump and continued, 'Yew mus be, cos ee said yew ad a miscarriage!'

Two other women turned to listen. Shell was reluctant, but also anxious to discover what he wanted.

'I… er… yeah… I'm er… I mean, I'm Shelly.'

She couldn't bring herself to say his name.

'Well, I gotta message from yewr usban: Sam's the

Man, ee sayz. Ee sayz ee'll wait f yew by the side entrance. Go an see im, love. I think ee's missin yew. Ave a quick one!'

'I don smoke.'

'Yew should, yewr lookin peeky.'

One of the others looked suspiciously at Shell. Someone from the estate, looked vaguely familiar.

'Ow come yewr in yer with a miscarriage, it don seem right t me!'

'Leave er be, Trace. She've bin through enough orready. Aven yew, love?'

But this Tracey examined her up and down and came to her own conclusion.

'I know, it musta bin a mistake. Typical Prince o Wales, eh? Always cock thin's up. My dad come in yer once f'r a knee operation an they done the wrong leg!'

Shelly nodded. She needed to act fast. Soon she might be discovered and the ward was full of busy-bodies.

'Yeah, yewr right. I'll go an see my Sam. Maybe ee'll get me onto another ward.'

She scuttled straight for the lift. It was incredible what a dressing-gown could do for you here: it was a security pass. She wondered which ward. Pressed a button at random. Numbers flicked on, off. Her plans: slip into a new identity. Adopt the girl. Avoid Sam, unless he proved he could be trusted. Release the flat. That was the aim. Everything else would follow.

She opened her eyes on what she thought was still her dream. It was her double, but not quite. The odd girl was wearing her clothes: black velvet, cream blouse and yet her scalpel features seemed ready to operate on Mary's brain. Then, when she smiled, it was her mam's mouth, kissing her to breathe again. Was this the wind to lift her up?

In the hothouse atmosphere of the ward she was stifled. She blinked to test the reality. The screen kept bleeping. No hint of air, except when this strange girl spoke soothingly, as though she'd always known her -

'Mary! We... I found yew see, by-a shops. I thought yew wuz dead. Yew look fine. It's so good t see yew got through it.'

'Ave yew come t take me away?'

Shell was stunned by this question. Here she was, tubed to a drip and wired to a screen, pale as a plaster Madonna, but contemplating escape, of all things.

'Mary.'

She held her hand as she had in the ambulance. Mary closed her eyes, saw her mam gripping tight along the pavement, worried at every passing car.

'We got so much in common.'

Mary observed the clothes, relieved that somebody had taken her shed skin.

'Yeah, I'm really sorry bout these,' Shell said.

Mary attempted a laugh, which ended as a choking fit. The monitor-line leapt and her tube almost detached. Shell placated her, afraid a nurse would come.

'Yer, take it easy!'

Mary's body was hollow. She must fill it with a new beginning. She held onto the coarse hand for guidance, croaking her words.

'I... don wanna go back!'

'Nor me... me neither! I never wanna go back. I wanna start summin really special.'

Mary was exhausted, her stomach scarred by sharp rock. This girl's energy could not be transfused, however tight her fingers locked. Her eyes pleaded to be let out.

'We'll do it, Mary, onest. Yew, me an... well, there's this bloke Sam. I don know bout im though. I gotta make shewer... Men. Yew carn tell with them, cun yew?'

He dialled the number, still unsure if he was doing the right thing. Maybe Castleton would seriously damage the girl. Did he want to be responsible for that? He thought of her fighting in the Royal and of the stinking subway and then of Shelly's single mindedness with that posh girl, staying with her when it made no sense to care.

'Ello? Ray Castleton yer, oo's that?'

'I...'

'Wha? What is it?'

His money ran out! Phoning a mobile was extortionate and he'd only cadged 20p from a smoking patient for a fag. That was it. Story of his life so far. He made no decisions. His lack of readies did it for him.

He even thought of contacting the Councillor fella. Get his name down the Civic Centre. Maybe he'd reward him. Two women, two ransoms and he hadn't kidnapped either of them!

No, he'd just go home and get grief from his mam, sullen indifference from his dad and abuse from John.

From the booth, he walked past the main reception towards the exit. He hated hospitals. As a kid he'd been to A & E a few times. Once his crazy dad had put a firework rocket in a glass jar as they had no milk-bottles. Splinters of glass had exploded and embedded in his legs. The Asian doctor had written down 'Accident with a bazooka' on his form. It became a family joke.

'Ey Sam! Sam the Man!'

He turned but could see nobody recognisable, only this smart girl. The overdose girl! She was up! Couldn't be! But Shelly's head on her body: a weird transplant. He was gobsmacked.

'Like it, eh?'

She spread her arms for admiration.

'Yew bloody nicked em off er? Is tha why yew wen with er? Bloody ell!'

'Don talk s soft! C'mon, come outside. Le's talk.'

They stood outside, well away from anyone, with the appearance of waiting for a lift. Shell cockily took his arm. Sam was uneasy.

'Well, we are married, in we? Arfta all, I didn ave yewr baby.'

'Give over, will yew. Ow d yew get them clothes anyway?'

'I stole em…'

'See…'

'I put em under my night-gown, walked inta the bogs like I woz really pregnant an give birth t this! Der-um!' she finished with a mock drum-roll.

'Yewer defnitlee off yewr trolley!'

'Look, Sam, yewr the Man, right? Waitin f me an all tha?'

'Well, aye…'

'Yew wanna go back t yewr mam an all them arguments, or join us?'

'Us? Oo's we…I mean us then?'

'Me an Mary, tha's oo!'

'So wha yew gunna do, rob a fuckin bank? Do a Bonnie n Clyde?'

'Sort of… not exaclee… See tha sky up there?'

'Eh?' Sam gazed upwards at the uniform grey wall of cloud.

'See tha sky. Well, we...I'm gonna change it. Paint over it. Make it worthwhile.'

Sam pulled away from her, itching from foot to foot, on the look-out for a taxi he couldn't afford. What was he doing chatting to this mad girl outside the Prince of Wales, when he could be delivering her back to her rightful place?

'Ave she got any money in tha jacket?' The plush velvet looked promising.

'Look, fuck yew Sam! I'm gunna do it without yew! We are!'

Now she was leaving him and striding off. All his chances disappearing again. He pursued her, lapping at her heels.

'Orright, Shelly, I'll do it.'

'Do what, exaclee? Do what?'

If he'd been tripping all this wouldn't have sounded so absurd. Shelly peered pointedly into his watery-blue eyes, testing.

'Yew know, whatever! Paint the fuckin sky.'

They folded up with giggling, supporting each other in case they collapsed in a tangled heap together.

'Fuckin funny way t be'ave, yew ask me!'

It was Tracey, the large and suspicious fag-smoker, come to light up, more public this time.

'An ow come yewr let out s bloody quick, eh?'

Shelly went up to her, full of daring now.

'We're avin another one, see. We jest decided... In fact, me an Sam'll jest go inside an book a room...I'll ave it underwater, tha way yew won yer the screams!'

As Shell and Sam danced off into the hospital, the buxom Tracey was left, mouth wide as the Bristol Channel.

'Fuckin mad, the pair of em! Fuckin off it!'

*

She was stabilising, the doctor told her. Soon she'd be off the drip and onto solids. She needed Shelly's hand once more, reassuring. She'd even ventured to the toilet, taking her contraption with her, a baby-walker without the sounds. She reached out and a hand caught hold of her. Seeing the dark uniform, Mary sprang away from it, stung.

'Hey, don't worry! It's okay!' The WPC leant over with a put-on smile

'Wha's up, wha's the matter?' Illogically, she thought of her father. Explosion at his factory.

'I was going to ask the same thing... Lissen, my name's PC Felgate. I'm here to help you out, that's all. You haven't done nothing wrong.'

'If I aven done nothin wrong then I musta done summin wrong!' She echoed her dad's annoying correction.

'Eh? Right, love... Just tell us your name for starters and where you live. That'll help us get you back home soon as poss.'

She was treating Mary like an infant.

'Don't know!' she replied accordingly.

The WPC tapped her pen on her notebook. Mary noticed her screen had blanked out. She sat up.

'D yew reckon coz my monitor's stopped that means I'm officially dead?'

WPC Felgate was getting impatient, she had drug-dealers to hunt down, burglars to question.

'It means you're very much alive... Now, how's about a little co-operation, love? Name and address please!'

'Okay, it's Shelly.'

'Shelly what?'

'Shelly Jones.'

'Jones? Well, it's better than Smith! Where do you

live Shelly?'

'43 Snowdon. On the estate.'

No sooner had she said it, than she knew it was a mistake. The policewoman would check and it would lead to Ant, who would deny any knowledge of a Shelly Jones.

The WPC continued her questioning.

'Look it's just routine, that's all. Are your parents likely to be there? Can I contact them?'

'No, I live there with my partner Anthony,' she tried to sound mature now. 'I really don wan yew t tell im. Ee's two-timed me, see. Tha's the whool reason I done this. I don wanna see im no more!'

Felgate looked at her rather dubiously, 'So your parents... Where are they?'

'Dead!'

'I'm sorry. Both of them?'

Mary nodded earnestly. She had never lied so much before and now she felt like she was digging her own grave.

'So who's your next of kin?'

She hesitated. As a young child she'd sometimes been melodramatic, anything to get her father's attention, a kiss or cuddle for the smallest pain.

'There's my uncle...'

'And his name is?'

She sat upright, beating one hand down onto here stomach, letting out strangled yell and convulsing - 'Yeeeeeeeeeeeeeeeaaaaaooowww!' She even frightened herself with it.

A nurse came to her assistance, asking the WPC to leave her alone. Mary groaned to add to the authenticity. *Casualty* had been her favourite series. Reluctantly, Felgate left. As the nurse fussed over her, muttering 'pain killers', she knew her time there was limited. She wished Shelly would return, though it occurred to her they had swapped identities. She needed to know more about who she was now, this Shelly Jones. It sounded tough and common. Ant would never mess with Shelly Jones. She'd show him.

Sam marvelled at this creature that proceeded to acquire a wheelchair in the same way he had swooped on his mam's handbag the day before. A day! It seemed more like a year! Not only that, but she'd been transformed from lousy larvae to bright butterfly.

She had even managed to lift a name-tag. They'd been walking along a corridor when Shelly had inexplicably shoved him towards a passing doctor. In the following ruck, as he whimpered many sorries, she must have whipped off the tag like a scrum-half picking out the ball.

Now Sam was full of admiration as she strutted with the name 'Mrs. G. Singh, Consultant Neurologist' attached to her lapel. Anyone less like a 'Mrs G. Singh' he couldn't imagine. But then, she could just be married to a Mr. Singh, couldn't she?

From being totally incongruous, Shelly had become a chameleon. She had seen this film once. At the time it was rubbish, but now it made sense. *Zelig* with Woody Something. About a man who changed appearances according to the background. As she breezily wheeled the chair without any protests, she even had second thoughts about her idea. She could remain in the Prince of Wales, as nurse, porter, or in Reception. Even taking over Mary's bed as a suicide attempt.

Towards the lift, Sam brought her down.

'Better take tha thing off, Shell!'

'Why?'

'Coz someone's bound t know er.'

She took his point and sadly unclipped her rise to power, popping it into her pocket for safe-keeping.

'Some ol wrinklie's gonna miss theyr wheelchair, y know.'

'They'll get another one.'

They were alone in the lift.

'So where we goin?'

'T see Mary. Let er out opefully.'

'No, I mean arfter. Wha's the big deal? Er dad's gunna find er. I'll get a lampin from my mam an yew…yew got nowhere t go.'

Shelly was on guard again. As the lift halted she stiffened, eyes alert.

'Ow the fuck d yew know wha I got an aven got, eh?'

Sam played with the card in his pocket, feeling along its sharp edges.

'I don mean nothin. Jest chill! I jest thought, y know…'

'Yeah, right… Anyway, if yewr in on this there's no messin, right?'

Sam took his hands from his pockets and displayed his palms in mock innocence.

'I dunno what yew mean!'

Shelly knew this would be the tricky bit, getting into the ward without causing a commotion. They were a couple now, her and Sam. Come to pick up their gran. Luckily, bed space and general chaos meant that Mary had been put in a ward with many geriatric cases. It was a pity that Sam resembled a grumpy scarecrow beside her Sunday best. He was jabbering even as they came to the ward doors.

'So wha if we get er out? Where we gunna go? Eh Shell?'

'Jest whisht will yew!'

'Whisht? What kind of a word's tha?'

'A good one.'

They waited a few minutes and, as expected, a patient ambled along and pressed the buzzer.

'Ey love, fancy a ride? It'll save yewr feet.'

The old man was jaded and grateful. He obligingly sat in their wheelchair. Sam was again impressed at Shelly, the great improviser. But once inside, he nervously glanced at doctors and nurses behind the desk. Shelly chatted casually to the patient.

'Nice t see yew got visitors at last, Ted!' a male nurse called out to the old man they pushed.

'I wish yew two were my grandchildren. I ardly ever see them. An my son don want t know me. Too busy with work, see.'

'Tha's a real shame! Wish I ad a granddad an all...Where to, love?'

Ted put out one arm like cyclist signalling. They passed Mary's section and Shelly made faces at her and mimed frantically. Mary was astounded. She couldn't thwart the giggles. They ached her insides like a stone rolling around. She glimpsed the boy, Sam, his hair brambly and expression harassed. She failed to interpret Shelly's signals, but was glad to see them approaching without the strange old man in the wheelchair. She had an awful feeling Shelly had picked up someone else along the way and he was part of her plan.

Mary flexed her right arm to show her freedom. She'd even eaten the soup, or so it was called: a dubious liquid with noodle-worms floating in it. It was visiting time, so they didn't stand out. She greeted them like two close friends.

'Hiya!'

Shelly sat down in the wheelchair.

'Hiya, Mare! Yew look a lot better! I couldn afford flowers, so I brought Sam. Yew cun sniff on im instead, eh Sam? '

She nudged him, but his eyes were treading the path out the window and away through the alleyways of Penybryn.

Mary sat upright, excited by the possibilities, afraid to make a new life.

'I'm Shelly now, see. Like yew! Ave a look at my chart.'

Shelly examined Mary's chart and read the name 'Shelly Jones' on top.

'Jones! Original!' she laughed.

Then Mary suddenly remembered the WPC and knew she'd return soon.

'Lissen Shelly, Sam... the police...'

Sam started. He looked at Mary for the first time properly, piercingly, ready to run.

'This constable. I give the wrong name an address an then faked a fit. Lissen... I wanna go with yew whatever. I know yew saved me an...'

'Yew don owe us nothin!' Sam was cutting.

'I don even know if I wanna live, but it's worth tryin summin else. There's no way back!'

'Tha's exaclee what I say. Le's get crackin!'

Shelly took control, pulling the curtains round and ordering Sam to help lift Mary onto the wheelchair. She produced the old dressing-gown from the bedside cabinet with a magician's flourish and Mary struggled to get it on. She slumped back and let herself drift. She had a strange vision of seeing herself running past her house with this same tatty gown on. Shelly yanked a blanket from the bed and draped it over Mary. All the while, Sam was flustering.

'Ow we gunna get er out, eh? This is bloody stewpid, yew ask me.'

Shelly saw the complications. More clearly, she saw beyond them. Sam annoyed her, but also made her wary. She peeped through the curtains. A policewoman was at the desk asking questions.

'Oh shit!'

Mary woke from her dreamy state, 'What? What is it?'

'It's that pig!'

For once Shell was stumped. Her eyes flittering like two birds seeking an opening. In a flash, she imagined Sam stealing the WPC's hat and legging it down the ward. She imagined Mary passing for an old lady, smothered in a shawl. Finally, she took the tag from her pocket and became 'Mrs G. Singh, Consultant' again.

'Stay put!' she commanded them.

She chose her moment just as Felgate was walking towards them. She emerged, an immature doctor, but with an air of desperate confidence.

'Have yew come to see Shelly Jones?'

Felgate read the tag. Doctors were getting younger and scrawnier by the day. Shell was putting on her best stage posh.

'Yes, I need to check out…'

'Well, she's had a relapse un-fort-une-ately. She can't see anybody now, I'm afraid. I am sorry.'

Shelly expected the WPC to be stroppy and was surprised with her compliance. In truth, she'd had a call about a missing girl, the daughter of a VIP and needed to follow up some leads on that. The station had received a call from the homes about some Shelly who'd caused trouble there and she guessed this was the one. There was no rush with her.

'Tell her there's no bother. I'll be back later.'

Out of the gates and down the hill. Mary was exhilarated. A breeze now: clouds sailing away overhead. She was cold and empty. She was full of air and light-headed. She couldn't believe how they'd done it.

'Jest takin er f'r a walk. Bit o fresh air. Orright?'

'Is that okay with yew, Shelly love?'

'Yeah, these re my best mates!'

'I'm not so shewer. I'll afto see a doctor.'

Soon as she left the desk, they were off. Through the security, down the lift, out the side entrance and across the car-park. It was like a ride on the shows. Sam sped on, altered now they were free.

'Off we go, down the road t Nowhere! But do I care? Do the fuck I care?'

Shell skipped and hopped along, giving out directions, till they came to a subway and Sam braked.

'No way! I int goin down there agen! Tha's where I met yew in-a first place. We int stayin down there!'

The breeze still blew, but now it brittled Mary's skin. Shelly climbed onto a bent street-sign. She became a speaker addressing them. Mary was fascinated by her sense of purpose. Sam let go of the chair, clouds in his eyes.

'Orright! This is where it ends...or begins. I'm a fuckin fugitive. We all are! Sam, yew cun either go back to yewr mam or come with me... Mary, we cun leave yew by yewr ouse no problem. I cun do it on my own, coz I'm goin to anyway. Whatever appens!'

Mary recalled the grip of hand, even though this girl

now reminded her more of her dad, the politician, than her gently caring mother. Sam looked puzzled.

'An what exaclee are yew gunna do? Yew still aven said. Maybe yew don even know!'

'Course I know, dull-doh! See them flats up there. She pointed at the houses and flats of New Pen, half of them rubbled.

'Well, I... we gunna take one over. It'll be easy enough. Then I'm gunna be like n urricane o colours through the estate.'

'Like a mobile rainbow, is it?' Sam mocked.

'What did yew say?' Mary couldn't believe it. Shelly was speaking her dream!

'Y know, like a strong wind colourin evrythin, evry blank wall an board an blind.'

Sam wished he was on something. He longed to trip and be that wind, blowing black, red, magenta, amber, all the colours and more, those without names. But he was so hungry. He'd stolen a couple of biscuits from the tea-trolley up the hospital, but now his stomach growled at him, a dog drooling to be fed.

'So wha yew gunna eat? Paint?'

Mary, however, was enchanted by Shelly's vision.

'I got nothin t lose. My boyfriend dumped me an my dad's got a girlfriend an forgotten all about my mam, like she never existed. I come second all the time! I'm with yew, Shell.'

'We'll problee on'y ave a short time before we afto move on. But there are other flats. One thin about Cwmtaff is, there's no shortage o empty buildins.'

Sam was tempted to leave them there, for the rough comfort of his own room and rougher tongue of his mam. He still thought of them as bounty and was attracted to this girl who seemed to be so determined, despite it all. Somehow, he'd already gone too far. The promise of a meal and he'd give it a trial.

Shelly was catching hold of the wheelchair, not waiting on his decision. As she steered it down the subway, her mad wildness was a magnet, drawing him on.

'We'll fuckin do it! Why not, eh? It's so fuckin mad it's gotta be better an chasin dead-end jobs all-a time.'

Shelly and Mary zoomed ahead.

'But!' he shouted, 'we gotta get food soon or I'll dig my teeth inta yew two!'

He held the notes tight, as he would a cue. The breeze seemed to change directions as he left the flats, tempting him this way or that. There were so many possibilities. But first, the munchies. Then what? He could return, pay off his mam. He could trade them in, make even more. He could blow it all on booze and tabs and win back Milky by treating him to a few pints. He could, could, could…

He felt like Shelly in her disguise as he wandered downhill and towards Cefn Road. Then he saw the cops! A patrol car slowed down opposite and he slunk the money into a pocket. They stopped and he continued, casually, trying to ignore them.

'Oi!' Eastenders talk.

'Yeah?'

'Over yer, mate!'

Two cops, one shaven-headed, the other young as him almost. He shuffled over. A photo of Mary.

'Seen this girl on the estate, ave you?'

'Nah! Sorry!'

He looked away up the road, gripping the notes in his pocket.

'Are you certain?' the younger one sounded posh.

'If you do, you tell us, orright? There's a reward!'

Mary was so attractive in the photo, so full of promise. He thought of the pale doll he'd left, blanketed in the wheelchair.

'Aye, no prob!'

They drove off and Sam sighed. Fags and food and then decide. The flat reminded him of dens they'd made up on Morlais Castle, the crypt their fortress. Squat was something the hippies did. A free for all. Free love. He imagined Shell painting his body and Mary bombing round in her wheelchair chanting, Chase me! Chase me!

Forty quid. It felt heavier than that. She even had her card in that velvet jacket. He was trusted.

'I've got plenty, yewr welcome to it!'

In the Spar, he caught himself wondering what the two girls ate, cursing himself because a reward and Ray Gun offered so much more. Still, he piled in fruit and other useless stuff, avoiding the Tampax, but putting in tissues as a concession. Six-pack of lager and Benson & Hedges to top the lot.

Outside, he scoffed the cold pasty and crunched crisps, his mouth a concrete-mixer. Meat sliming down his throat and pastry like putty tasted like a gourmet's delight. They'd have to eat their finger-nails till…

Again, he was on the wrong track. He was going soft. Down Cefn Road to Shell's old place. Telephone kiosk not far from the Catholic Church. By then he'd know, one way or the other. He weighed it up: in one hand Ray Gun's card, in the other the money (what was left of it). Castleton would cut her up, or his cronies would. Deliver Mary back to her dad and he'd make a fuss for a while and then what had she said? She'd end up second best.

For the first time in his life, Sam Taylor felt

responsible for other human beings. He was frightened, but also grateful. He enjoyed the power and it terrified him. He wanted a sign, but none arrived. He hesitated at the phone, saw himself working for Castleton as a courier, or even dealer, with money not a problem to constantly bother his head.

The top-floor landing was dark and depressing. A stench of piss like school toilets. Squashed and dented cans littered the floor. Nobody lived at this level now, that's why Shell had chosen it. Nobody directly below to pick up sounds either. Just a few flats left on the ground floor.

Mary sat in her wheelchair dozing. Shell was uncomfortable in her clothes now, like she'd stolen the girl's personality and left her with nothing. Hunger had caught up with her and she wished she'd asked Sam to bring some food before he got the rest of the stuff. She kicked at the wooden-boarded door. Maybe she could be resourceful, like some castaway, and make a tool out of a can to prise off those boards?

Even here, where nobody went, there was graffiti. The walls told a grim story, secrets like toilet walls:

If you want it up the bum call

DONNA IS A DOG SLAGG BITCH

Dust flew as her shoes scuffed.

'C'mon Sam! C'mon, urry up mun!' Her stomach moaned at her like her mam on a downer.

'Shelly, carn yew clear up this mess?'

Her mess. Her chaos. Her toys of destruction. Syringe and chemical. Inoculated into ignorance.

Mary stood on the flat roof, naked. The wind supported her. Below her she could sense, though not see, chimneys dragoning fire. She flapped her arms frantically, wishing to fly. Nothing happened. Behind her, her father's voice was imploring yet distant.

'Mary! Get dressed will you? This is no time for this silly attitude!'

She turned to reply, but he was nowhere to be seen. Only an opening into the roof, like a periscope.

The wind still held her, a figure-head on a ship. The chimneys warned her, but soon the fire would spread and the whole building would go up.

From out of the opening came a long snake of red. It slithered across the roof to Mary's feet, tripping her up, so that she fell back, became part of it. She was stuck to its glutinous texture, its smell swallowed her whole. It was a bed and a suffocating plastic bag. It was a refuge and a coffin.

Sam lay on Shell's bed about to light up, when he sniffed. Definitely gas. He went to the window and rammed it open.

'Pissin ell! Carn even ave a fag!'

He rummaged through her belongings. Everything was haywire and nothing looked worth taking back. He eventually fished out a pair of black knickers and fell onto the bed again. He tested their elastic, pulling it taut then letting it go like a catapult. They had silver stars on them. He put them to his nose and thought of Shelly. He recalled her putting on the ones he'd stolen, but kept being drawn down the subway to the bundle she'd been before.

He undid his trousers and unzipped himself. He shouldn't be doing this. He should be moving on. He smoothed the knickers across his cheeks so it could be anyone they belonged to and felt his prick harden, his hand rubbing against it to make it spring.

The door swung open like a cowboy saloon.

'I knew yew'd come back yew...'

Sam stuffed the knickers down his trouser-front and sat up. At the door was Castleton, already unbuttoned and zip half undone, in a farcical mirror-image of Sam. Sam put his knees up to hide his shame. Castleton propered himself and glared at Sam.

'What the fuck?'

'Mr Castleton! I... I tried t phone yew earlier. I found er. I woz lookin f yew. I'll bring er. She's in the ospital. She tried t top erself,' Sam babbled as Castleton fumed and soon stood over him. He extracted the knickers from their hiding-place and held them out: exhibit A.

'Yew! What the fuck re yew doin yer? It's breakin an entrin, tha's what it is. I'll ave yew put away fr this yew little perve... What is it with girl's knickers, eh? Do yew jest go round town collectin em, or wha? I give yew my fags an yer yew are on my fuckin property, avin a fuckin wank all over this lovely bed. Yew'd better ave a fuckin good reason or yewr dead, right. Dead!' Ray Gun spat out every syllable. Sam wished Shelly were here to dig him out.

'I ...er... said... Mr Castleton... I got er key... I wuz waitin f yew, t tell yew. I'll get er yew t night.'

Sam felt Ray Gun's eyes interrogating, even when he avoided them. Next instant, he was pushed backwards, lying prostrate, with Castleton stab-poking each word at him.

'Right! Yew got one more chance cunt-face! Yew bring tha slag back yer or yewr dead meat. Yer it? I int even that bothered bout er tell the truth, but she owes me money an nobody gets away from theyr fuckin debts, see? Got it? '

Sam knew. His mind was made up as Ray Gun's eyes lasered into him, burning holes in his brain.

'Mr Castleton… I'm really sorry! She's yewers. I'll ave er yer no problem.'

She watched as Mary woke, stirring, pushing off the blanket. She saw herself earlier that day, limp and vulnerable, nightdress and gown; no protection. She went over and grasped Mary's hand again, this time tickling her palm gently, like an infant's. Mary's eyes were still out at sea.

'Yew could've done with that!'

'What? What's the matter, Mare?'

'Red paint. I ad a dream. It would've bin perfect!'

'Shush now, take it easy.' Shelly soothed her hair away from her face. Mary was so earnest, a smile would split her in half. 'Yew ungry? I'm fuckin starvin! I hope Sam aven done a runner with yewr cash. I don trust im really. Maybe it's jest coz ee's a fella.'

'I know what yew mean!'

'Sorry, I don need t tell yew, do I? Avin said tha, my mam ad no shape on er, so I carn be sexist, can I?'

'Yewr mam?'

'Dead, like yewers. OD'd on-a ard stuff. Carn say I miss er though. I woz stuck in-a Omes.'

'Sorry.'

A clanking up the stairs. Shell looked for a weapon. If it was the police… She jumped behind the wheelchair, now a chariot. But the clanking soon became Sam's voice cursing his way up. He collapsed onto the landing in a jumble of suitcase, spade and shopping, taking deep breaths and gobbing onto the dirt-matted floor. Cans of lager rolled out and joined their empty cousins.

Mary began to laugh, then held her mid-riff. Shelly giggled a fit.

'Spade! Yew thinkin bout startin a fuckin roof-garden or wha? '

'Fuck... phhhhhhh... off!'

'I see yew got all the essentials, Sam, like bloody booze an gardnin gear!'

Shell dived down onto the shopping bags and hauled out a packet of crisps, tearing it open and stuffing her face. Half way through she guiltily offered some to Mary, who declined.

'My guts re terrible! I think they musta pumped them out with evrythin else.'

Sam cracked open a can and slumped against a wall, getting his breath back. Shelly inspected his goods.

'Well, spade's better than fuckall. It'll do!'

'Ow d yew mean, it'll do? I risked my life f that... I skanked it out of ower back garden an my darlin bro seen me, didn ee? Mam's gonna kill yew, ee sayz... I'm diggin my own fuckin grave I tell im! Oh, an by the way, I got yewr clothes, lovely black knickers...I tried em on.'

After a last laugh, Shelly was all action, 'Le's get inside. We gotta find out what ower Pentouse Suite is like... chase away the rats, that kinda thin.'

Mary edged her wheelchair near the door. She wasn't sure if she was still 'Shelly Jones' or not, whether she had died and been re-born.

'We ought to ave a ceremony.'

'What?' asked Shell.

'Y'know, like launchin a ship. The openin of a door to a new life.'

'Fuck! I'm all f that!'

Sam took out his prick and blessed the door with a stream off piss.

'Well, it's yewr terrortree now, is it Sam? Put that thing away, will yew. Yew don wanna give Mary yer a relapse, d yew?'

Sam struggled and sweated with the spade. The head loosened and the shaft began to split.

'Why the fuck d they bother? Oo wan's t live yer?'

'We do!'

Shelly always had an answer.

Mary thought of her dad, how he'd be panicking. His name in the papers. Daughter missing. Bad for the image.

The flat was as gloomy and damp as they'd expected. No rats, but a musty tomb. Its darkness made Mary want to rise up, break the window-boards and let light in. It was empty apart from a single blotched mattress and, absurdly, a large glass vase. Shell and Sam hunted in and out the rooms. No electric. No water. Amazingly, a toilet and bath intact.

For some reason lines kept coming into Mary's head. She couldn't stop them: 'Home is a grave where I belong' and 'At least I'll be buried with friends'.

Shell laid the shopping out on the draining-board.

'Bananas! Good stuff! Honeydew melon, nice one… no knife…we'll afto t ewse the spade… Condoms, eh? Really ewseful. I know a nice recipe. They taste a bit like squid.'

Sam went over to investigate, like he'd forgotten what he bought.

'Condoms? Piss off! What I shoulda bought woz some tab's up-a Pen Inn. That way we could at least bring some light t this dump!'

Shelly swung to face him, full on, yelling – 'No fuckin drugs, right? No way! I seen enough of that!

Yew wanna drop that shit, yew cun fuck off. Right?'

Sam shrugged and backed off. 'Orright, Shelly! Cool ead! I'll jest afto survive on booze an se… well, booze anyroad.'

Shell had liberated the flat, let in what light was left on this strangest of Sundays. She had managed to edge the bathroom window open and creak at gaps in the boards, till one fell off. She hoped nobody was passing below or they'd have been knocked out. She lay in the bath on a bed of dead flies, her feet on the taps, and felt a sense of achievement. It was peaceful at last after Sam's tantrums. It bugged her: would she confront him or not? Make him confess?

Mary was sleeping in her wheelchair after nibbling unconvincingly on a banana. Sam had generously suggested she could take the mattress.

'Tha's really kind of yew Sam. Didn know it woz yewr flat.'

'Look, loosen up Shelly! I didn mean it like tha… Look… tell yew wha…' he paced around, avoiding eye-contact, 'I'll even throw in an electric blanket!'

Shell sat cross-legged, taking in his movements.

'Electric blanket, eh? Where's tha?'

'Yer, ocourse!' he stopped toing-and-froing and proudly puffed out.

'Piss off, Sam!'

'Charmin, Shell! Look at all I done f yew All's I wan is a bit of a cwtch.'

Shelly got up and sway-hipped towards him provocatively.

'Sam? D yew fancy me or wha?'

Sam gaped gullibly.

'Aye… Well…'

88

'Well stop hidin yewr spade down yewr jeans, dig an ole an jump in it!'

'Fuck off then!' he shouted and stormed into the bedroom, throwing himself onto the mattress and remaining face down.

'I might not stay yer anyway! If I'm gunna be treated like shit, I might as well be treated like shit in the comfort of my own ome.'

Shell went in to talk, but he was already asleep and snoring. She spotted a business-card on the floor by the mattress. Must've fallen from his pocket. She picked it up. Ray Castleton! So Sam was one of his errand boys. But why hadn't he turned her in? After all, he'd had lots of opportunities.

In the bath, she burnt the edges of the card with matches he'd bought. They could escape, her and Mary, into the night. The police would be crawling over Pen though. A Councillor's daughter gone missing. Boyfriend living on the estate.

She could test him or display the evidence. Was Castleton on his way at this very moment? She blew out the match and went to get the spade. The door was open, no protection. She lifted the glass vase and placed it above the ajar bathroom door, got back into the bath and clutched the spade like a comforter to a child. She heard screaming from below on the street and her bladder was a needle jabbing within.

She pissed into the waterless toilet. It was silent outside now. She couldn't sleep as her mind busied itself with thoughts of graffiti. She saw a grey ray gun broken in two and the point of a shell (was it called a whelk?) coming down from the sky into the gap between its halves. She saw an ant with a smug face crushed by a wheel. Above all, she imagined flames, phoenix flames rising, but out of them came... It had

89

to be a horse for Mary, a seashell for her and... What for Sam? A card? A card that was burning. She smelt smoke. She blew its ash. It settled on her like a nagging reminder.

The first place must be the shops. Where the shutters on Mary's eyes had gone down. They would announce themselves to Penybryn. They'd bring down the sun. Seize the sky.

Mary woke into the tomb darkness. Cupboard in her parents' room. Hide n seek. Her mam after her. Don't breathe! She stretched her arms out. No clothes hanging and no door. There was a rustling, a scratching and scraping sound.

'Mam?' she whispered.

The cold ran through her veins, her blood transfused into icy water. The air choked, filling her lungs with stale stench. She spluttered and the scratching turned into two shapes she could just make out, scurrying by her feet. Along her spinal cord, fear pulled taut.

Rats! Rats big as cats. No Pied Piper here. No cupboard and no mam. She wasn't Mary buried alive, but Shelly Jones in a wheelchair.

Rats! What did they find to eat here? The floorboards? Probably Sam's discarded crisp-packet. A mischief of rats. Trivia. She knew that! What an understatement.

A police siren rang out from the mazy estate. She couldn't stay and she couldn't go back. This place was a slum, but at least there was Shelly, who seemed so full of possibilities. Even Sam – who wasn't her type, was just the sort her dad would disapprove of, call a 'waster'. She'd been there before, wouldn't again. But no harm in a friend.

She felt pangs of hunger for the first time since her suicide attempt. She was so weak she could hardly shift the wheels. She rubbed at them and they squeaked back, like rodents. As she began to move, she heard footsteps wandering the flat. She tried to lift herself. The police, come to drag her back! Arrest the others for kidnapping. Back to her dad's – first fussing, then his second marriage: she the reluctant bridesmaid.

Sam woke up with a hard-on. In a flat with two girls, but nowhere to go. He took out Shell's black knickers and put them over his face like a mask. He breathed them in and out. Perhaps he was becoming a pervert? He certainly had to make do with Shelly's underwear. She was like a fridge on legs.

He checked his other pocket for the card. Gone! He fingered through each pocket in panic. He crawled from the mattress and felt blind over the floorboards for it. Not a sign!

His hard-on had deflated like a punctured balloon. He desperately needed a piss now, but couldn't risk waking Shelly. He could go in the sink. He remembered the matches in the kitchen as well. He bluffed towards the wall and palmed along to find the door.

In the kitchen, the sink was too high. He'd end up soaking the only clothes he had and mankin of piss. His hands stumbled to the shelf. The glass vase was missing, as were the matches. What was Shelly doing with strikes and a vase? Making a petrol bomb?

By now, he was busting. About to wet himself! Sam the Man? Sam the Baby, more like.

'What the fuck!'

He edged the bathroom door open slowly.

Something fell! He leapt back like an electric shock. An explosion of glass, splinters and shards flying like shrapnel.

'Jesus fuckin Christ, Shelly! Yew tryin t kill me?'

She was on all fours slithering in red paint. It was a concrete slope, but the paint kept flowing like a fountain. He was somewhere behind her. Castleton. She could hear his deep breathing, but he hadn't managed to catch her. She could make out the end of the slope, but somehow knew it was followed by a vertical drop which she had to risk. She was soaked in paint, it seeped into her clothes, saturating them with its heaviness.

Out of nowhere, she was bitten! Some insect stabbed at her cheek. She slapped at it, but it was gone, cried out in pain.

'Aaaaaaaaaaaaaaagh!'

Figure at the door. Must be Ray Gun. The spade. She raised it to club the intruder. Her dream a prophecy. The bastard!

Just as she was bringing it down, Sam stepped out of Castleton's shape. Thwarted the blade.

'Shell, it's me! What yew doin? Yew fuckin mental or wha? Jesus Christ, yewr covered in blood. I'm sorry Shell, but yew shouldn ave put…'

In the dawn light squinting through window-gaps, she saw his stricken expression. The vase fragmented at his feet. She felt her face and extracted a small needle of glass. Her knickers and skirt were sopping with blood, which ran down her legs like that fountain.

'Sorry Shell, but I gotta…'

Sam tip-toed to the toilet, pissed into the empty pan. His shrivelly-scared prick made her chuckle inwardly, despite all the chaos. Then she remembered. She found the card: black-edged and blood-stained.

Sam shook himself and fussed over her.

'Shell, where's the cut? Yew got blood all over. We gotta get yew up the ospital quick!'

Shelly waved the card at him, as if he were the pesty insect. He backed off.

'It's my time o the month, Sam, yew little prick… In evry sense o the word! Ow come yew ad this, eh? What yew doin f Castleton, eh? Runnin errands, is it?'

They heard Mary's wheelchair cranking towards them from the living-room. It crunched over the broken glass which had spread far.

'Wha's goin on?'

Sam gave her space to enter. She saw the blood, spade still held be Shelly, the broken vase and Sam, with flies undone. She saw the raised card, but couldn't make out its print.

'Sam! What ave yew done to er, yew bastard? What ave yew done?'

She hauled herself from her chair to accost him and was falling backwards till he grabbed her and tried to put her back. Her fists blew weakly at his head. She sat back exhausted. Shelly still brandished the card like court evidence.

'Well? Fuckin explain this if yew cun!'

Sam turned towards the window, seeking some hope of escape. He did up his zip, then faced the two girls. The truth wasn't his natural territory, but he'd made the decision when Castleton had threatened him, so now to convince them.

'Orright! This is the fuckin truth, the whool truth, so elp me G…'

'Bet yew don even bleeve in im,' interrupted Mary.

'Spit it out!' said Shelly.

'Yesterday mornin, before I met yew in-a subway, Shell... I come across im. Ee give me is card, tol me t look out f yew. Promised me money, even a job... Well, when I wen' back f yewer clothes ee woz in yewer bedsit. Ee threatened me. Tol me if I didn get yew to im, I'd be dead meat. So...'

He searched their faces for a glimmer of support. Both stared cynically.

'So, I... I decided ee wuz a fuckin wanker! Ee treated me like shit, so ee musta done worse...'

'Yeah, on'y tried t rape me, tha's all!'

'Look, Shell, I've ad loadsa chances t give yew up.'

'Ee could still be lyin, Shelly.'

Shell arrow-eyed his face, delving deep into his grey eyes for a hint of lies.

'Shelly, we gotta get yew cleaned up!'

For the first time since the pub, she was touched by him. If he was genuine it was a real risk. Ray Gun had spies everywhere. Sam would either deliver her or be cut up. That was the score.

After she'd eaten some cereal, Mary summoned up strength to dress. The other two had managed to squeeze gaps in the boards, so more light entered. The thought of rats didn't put her off her food.

Sam had offered to help her, but Shelly bossed him out to buy Tampax and paint in that order

'Tampax?' he'd protested, 'I carn buy them, I'm a fuckin man!'

'Coulda fooled me! Nick em then!' Shell suggested.

'Oh, orright!'

Shell gave the best of her clothes to Mary, but nothing fitted. She needed a crane to get into Shelly's old jeans.

'Yew'll jest afto stay an invalid in a wheelchair then, won' yew?'

Finally, she found a denim skirt which she strained into, leaving the top button undone and an oversized blouse, which Shelly mysteriously claimed wasn't hers anyway and probably belonged to the previous owner of the bedsit.

Mary was a scruffbag, but content enough. No essays. No exam worries. No dad to trample down her mam's memories. Shelly Jones was a tight fit, but at least she could breathe easily. There were search-parties out for Mary, but she'd left her there, by the shops, the empty carcass of her former self.

He felt like he'd had half a bottle of gin over his Crispies, but it had only gone to his eyes. In his blurry vision, the estate was bandaged up, but he was still wary. The cops wouldn't give up and his disguise wasn't that convincing: Mary's reading-glasses and Shell had done a quick grease job on his hair, though he daren't ask what she'd used for the slick-back effect. It was better than her first suggestion—

'If yewr so moithered bout buyin Tampax, why don yew dress up in drag? It'd sewt yew, Sam. Yew'd make a lovely woman!'

'Tha's the on'y way I'll get inta yewr knickers anyroad!'

'Oh! Ark at frustration case. Anyway, where're my black ones? Yew still aven give em back! Yew wearin em, Sam?'

Teasing him got him all the more excited. Sooner or later, he thought. When she comes off it. He'd kept Ray Gun's card, assuring the girls he'd phone with a false lead.

Now he touched the hard plastic of Mary's credit card and chanted her number to himself: 7248... 7248... 7248... He shouldve scribbled it on his hand. Past the graffiti-ridden bus-shelter, he tried to see himself in the plastic window. There was no reflection. Maybe he'd become a vampire overnight. He sniffed the bloodied card and it reminded him of Shell. He imagined himself as the kind he'd spew on: studious specs and chippy hair, stubble since Saturday and a lingering smell of what he'd call "gypo".

As he rounded the corner, he caught the yellow flash of a police-car coming up the hill from the Park. With perfect timing, he disappeared into the very subway they'd met. There, he half-expected to discover another body stirring in the darkness. But it was deserted, except for memories. It was astounding to think how broken and fragile she'd seemed then and how in control she was now. How could it be the same person?

He lit up and savoured a fag, throwing the ignited match into a neglect of litter. Flames refused to rise in the prevailing damp. He sucked on the possibilities... Booze and tab's down the pub... Shell would murder him...Was he married already? Ray Gun's mates could be there, anyway... Pay back his mam. Clean up. Say he'd got a job. Staying over at Milky's... Nick paint from his dad's shed. Bound to be old cans there.

He must be mad. The cops could pick him up and charge him with abducting Mary. Maybe the hospital had given descriptions and the police made connections. Might even think he had kidnapped her to demand money from her well-off daddy. He had to be crazy, staying with a runaway no-hoper and a failed suicide.

Out from his burrow, he made for Beacons Road

and the small branch of Lloyd's there. When he keyed in Mary's pin of 5468 it came up as 'INVALID'.

'Shit!' er dad had probably cancelled it already. Then he tried another combination and it worked. He felt like a criminal, with £200 on the screen enticing. But he decided on £100, with £40 for his mam and £60 for the Tampax How much did they cost anyway? Besides, they needed more food, soap and things like that.

In the Spar, he concealed the Tampax under a loaf of bread, deciding not to nick it with his hundred rolled up. But when it came to the box, the assistant kept putting through the bar-coder and no price came up. She hailed another assistant, tidying shelves –

'Ey, Katie! Ow much is this Tampax?'

Sam could've hidden behind the stacked cans of beans, he was so embarrassed. Sweat prickled his forehead and the grease melted. It always seemed to happen to him. Once he was buying condoms in Boots which were on offer and the till-girl had even called the manager on the shop Tannoy to check the price.

Later, he plucked up enough courage to phone Castleton's mobile from the kiosk. It galled him to waste a pound.

Castleton sounded flustered. 'Yes?'

'It's me… Sam… member? I wuz arfter tha Shelly.'

'Well, where is she?'

'She done a runner from ospital. I did try t…'

'Yew shoulda phoned me las night. I know she's on'y a little slag, but she owes…'

He was cut off. Sam hoped it was enough, but doubted it. The glasses had begun to give him a headache. It was like the morning after, without the night before! He turned up the Avenue towards the estate. After that, it was up Snowdon, before a gwli leading to his house and over the back into the garden.

Outside one detached house with a semi-circular drive, he heard raised voices and could make out a man and woman in anxious conversation. The man was getting into a brand new BMW, while the woman held onto the door.

'What's the point, Frank? The police will handle it!'

'I don't care! It's the least I can do for her! I've neglected her too long, that's the truth of it!'

Sam made the connection and wanted to take off Mary's glasses, in case they recognized them

Outside a house along the sweep of Snowdon Road was a police-car. Nothing unusual around these parts, but Sam still made a connection. It was coincidence after coincidence! He crossed the road and looked away from that house.

Further up the road, a boy passed him. He resembled one of John's friends, but luckily didn't speak. Some Goth adorned in black eye-shadow. Sam attempted the hard look, but it was difficult wearing girl's glasses and with chip-fat layering his locks.

The door on their back fence was open, but the shed padlocked. He didn't know why, as anything valuable had been skanked. They'd discovered some boys once nicking the garden furniture and one was a Richards (the family who ruled the estate like a mini-mafia). His dad had pretended to chase them, but Sam knew he was petrified. The Richards did what they wanted. Cross them, you were cut up.

As Sam rattled the padlock, his mam came pounding out from the kitchen armed with a frying-pan. She was just about to launch into him.

'Mam, it's me, Sam!'

He thrust his hand into his pocket, grabbed a wad of notes and offered them, like a guilty husband with flowers. She lowered the pan and eyed her wayward son, oddly bespectacled and dripping with globules of thick sweat.

'Sam? Where the ell ave you been? You looks terrible. You on drugs, or what?'

'Mam! Yers yewr money, take it! I'm dead sorry, mam, I'm sorry!'

She was about to cwtch him, but didn't like the look of that stuff dripping from his head. It was like his brain was melting. Which shouldn't take long, she thought.

'Oos glaasses you got on?'

'It's my disguise, mam. I'm tryin t look brainy!'

'Brainy? More like a drip with that stuff comin outa your ead!'

Then they laughed in unison. They laughed together like they hadn't done for years. Not since Sam had drawn wrinkles on his dad's forehead as he sat drunk at Christmas. His dad snored and the wrinkles wriggled like caterpillars. As they laughed Sam wondered if he'd come home for good. How could he return to that cold, damp derelict flat?

"Squat" was an ugly word. Mary had said it reminded her of toads in a poem. To Shelly, this was their place, however sordid. And even the rats didn't deter, so she'd said, 'Lovely! Fried rat, my favourite!' They'd giggled till Sam made some stupid remark about already eating it "down the chinky".

It was like opening up a coffin lid to find the corpse still breathing and reviving it with laughter and conversation. If they had to go, there were other places to free. She thought of the boarded-up Club down town, even the totally run-down old Town Hall. They could move on to mansions from this lowly beginning.

With the spade she prised the boards, letting more of the sky in. Seizing it with both palms, the light a precious currency. It entered and rested on Mary, snoozing again in her wheelchair.

Shell felt weakened by her period and exertions to get clean. She worried about Sam. Wondered if he would betray them. She thought about the paint, hoping he'd bring back black and white. A tribute to Mary on the wall where she'd collapsed: white pills like UFOs wanting to abduct her, yet below a shell twisting like a horn and out from it fire flaming the flying pills upwards and away.

As she stared at Mary, the sun seemed to kindle flames in the girl's cheeks. Her pallor turning to a promise of summer.

When Mary woke she thought she was in hospital. The heat blanketed her and the window was a blurry vision. For a moment, she fancied it was all a dream: the escape and the dingy flat.

Then she saw Shelly squatting on the grimy floorboards. She was animated, but completely focussed. Mary didn't want to disturb her with speech. She was like a child discovering a new skill, her right hand shading and her head shifting through angles.

Mary felt at home for now, slimmed into this identity. She'd make her dad suffer, as Anthony had made her suffer. She'd make him anxious whether she was alive or dead.

She spoke at last, intrigued, 'What is it?'

Shelly started. She had forgotten Mary was there at all she was so intense.

'It's an idea, tha's all… Course, we'll afto agree, I spose.'

'Agree on what, Shelly? Yewr sooo mysterious.'

Shell put down the pen and left her work. She was back to her other self, a whir of energy. She stood over Mary, amazed to see her clothes pressing into a body so unlike her own.

'Tell me, Mare. Tell me what ee done t yew. Tha boy.'

'Anthony?'

'Yeah!'

'Ee two-timed me. I wuz left waitin f im. Ee never come.'

'The bastard! We got so much in common, Mary... I mean, ower mams... an we both bin shat on.'

Mary wished she were a child again. To be pushed from place to place, to be fussed over. She didn't want to be a teenager. She didn't want to spit out her past, however vile it tasted.

'Tell me bout yewr drawin Shell. What's it of?'

Shelly drew back, turning into the sunlight.

'It's crap! I wuz never any cop at art.'

'C'mon, don be darft! Le's ave a look!'

As Mary feebly wheeled herself towards the paper, Shelly snatched it up. She eclipsed the sun from Mary totally, a dark silhouette over her. If only she would pull Mary up and hold her, close and warm in the flat's sharp air. Instead, Shelly stooped to her level and tentatively unveiled the drawing. Mary squinted at the sudden brightness.

'I tol yew it wuz crap!'

Mary saw round shapes and jumping lines. She could clearly distinguish a perfect shell.

'No, it's good. What is it?'

'It's f yew. It's jest a plan. I'll tell yew later.'

'There yew go agen, Mystic Meg!'

Shelly was up once more and twirling the drawing

from Mary's grip. She rolled it like a scroll.

Mary managed to stand up and stumble into the bathroom. The toilet stink reminded her of Ant after too many beers and a takeaway. For the first time since her attempt at suicide, she felt a need for home comforts. The dirt seemed to seal her pores, so they couldn't breathe. She turned the taps in hope and groaned. Never thought of water as a luxury! Sam probably hadn't bought any either. Only the humiliation of struggling back home, a lost and sorry child, prevented her from leaving. What she desired, Shelly couldn't give. What Shelly sought was nothing Mary could help her find.

Only down the road, a bus-ride away. No, she could free-wheel there! Her dad's pity. Bath and bed beckoned. But the piles of notes and deadlines on her calendar were a dead weight and dates of her failure.

Sam sat back in the opulence of an armchair. It was tempting, staying put. It would be so easy. He slurped tea and stuffed himself with fruit-cake, as his mam examined him closely for any evidence of drug-taking.

'You gets ungry after that wacky stuff, don't you?'

'What yew on bout, mam?'

'Anyway, evryone's concerned about you all of a sudden. I've ad that Milky ringing up. Sounded drunk to me – an goin on about his girlfriend's clothing you took. Sam, you're not in trouble, are you? All this disguise business.'

'Yeah, I'm wearin er clothes, in I?'

She chuckled, becoming serious in a second.

'An some bloke called Castleton phoned. Says ee needs to talk to you desperate. Bout some girl or summin? I don't like the sound of it, son!'

'Castleton? Oh shit! Ow did ee find my number?'

Sam sprung up and peered through their front window, half-expecting Ray Gun and his heavies at the door. He drummed an irritating rhythm on the sideboard, as he'd done on many a school desk.

'Mam!' his voice cracked to a high pitch, 'if ee calls, tell im I've left town, right? Ad t go away t work. Orright?'

His mam shook her head, 'I don't like it, Sam. What's goin on? You takes 20 quid from me an gives me 40 like some bribe. Are you dealin? Is that it? Are you dealin for this Castlehead? Ave you gone off with his money?'

He stood behind her, not wanting his eyes to confess.

'Look mam! Yew bin watchin too much *Eastenders*. There's no hassle. I gotta place t live, I gotta girl, see. Ewsed t go with im. I borrowed the money off er an I'll pay er back like I done with yew. I'm gettin sorted, mam, onest I am.'

He was becoming more like Shelly every minute, with the tales he made up. Unexpectedly, his mam's plump body shook with a fit of giggles.

'I bin watchin too much? You're a larf Sam! You comes out with the plots of the laast 20 episodes an I bin watchin too much!'

A strange car drew up outside their house.

'Mam, I'm not yer member? I'm in England workin. Better still, Scotland.'

A man got out, dressed in a suit. Not Castleton, but Sam was spurred into action.

'I'll jest get some clothes t gether... an some paint if tha's...'

'Paint?'

'Aye! Do the flat up like.'

'You needs a good wash first.'

'Aven got time, mam. Sorry, mam, sorry!'

He kissed her on the forehead. She wiped off the spots of grease.

'Member, I'm not yer, right?'

'Not yer? You never woz yer, Sam! Never ave been.'

'Mam, mam! There's summin up! My thingy's bleedin!'

Her mother was only half-conscious, draped over the sofa, some fella all over her. Shelly was desperate for help, but she ignored her pleas.

'It's orright, Shelly. Don be s silly, it's on'y women's problems.'

'But I int no woman. I'm a girl!'

Her mother slurred, barely able to focus.

'Get a load o bog-roll an shove it up yewr pants. That'll last till I cun sort yew out.'

Now she bled just as much, loathing it as she had always done. A sign of weakness.

From down the stairs in one of the occupied flats, came sounds of activity; furniture dragged and hectic voices on the edge of arguments. A removal van drew up outside and the men entered the building.

It would all end soon. The last few families would pack up and go and the whole block would be ready for demolition. One less flat-full of problems for Penybryn; one more rectangle of broken stone where they'd been.

Right in the middle of the main road to the hospital she saw it, a fountain of red like a firework, but with drops of blood cascading, not sparks from gunpowder. The next sketch was growing in her head. Sam must bring red.

*

Mary felt superfluous, as Shelly busied in the kitchen, preparing a paltry meal. She didn't really want to return, but she had no choice. She couldn't survive like this. She pushed herself onto the landing, not even considering the stairs. She halted at the top. She could launch herself off, but she would tumble, injure herself and end up back in hospital. It was like a game of snakes and ladders, only it was life.

'Oh fuck!' her voice sounded louder than she expected, reverberating down towards the family on the move.

Shelly came running and was clearly annoyed, 'What the ell yew doin? Tryin t get us caught, or wha?'

'Shelly, I gotta go! I'm no ewse to anybody!'

She felt tears rise up, a spring she couldn't resist. It was a relief, but if only Shelly would drink them deep.

'Ey! an all-a time I thought we'd got no water! Yew've solved ower problem, Mary. See, yew are ewseful, arfta all.'

Mary quaked, half-laughing and half-crying. Reluctantly, awkwardly, Shelly caught hold of her, smoothing her hair away from the tears.

'Mary, love, it's really up t yew. Yew gotta decide, but maybe yew could give it a chance?'

Mary wanted more. She wanted to be told why.

'Yew got nothin t lose. I got evrythin…'

'Yeah? A bastard of an ex an a dad oo don give a fuck! Evrythin?'

She was explaining why not, but not giving her a reason. If Shelly had kissed her then, even on the cheek, it would have explained so much. But Shelly spun her round.

'Sam'll be back soon. We'll all talk! I got plans. C'mon Mare, we're the Fugitive Three, eh? Tears on tap.'

*

He unlocked the padlock. His mam had given him the key. There was nothing worth skanking in the shed, but even nothing wasn't safe round here. As he opened the door, which was split anyway, toilet rolls toppled to his feet. He couldn't believe it! It was a sanctuary for assorted bog-rolls: stacked on dust-smothered shelves, in buckets, even balancing on the prongs of a fork. The dilapidated rabbit-hutch was home to several pink and yellow ones. It was like they'd been breeding here. Many were soggy and sad. A few recent ones stood out for their whiteness and prime positions on a rack of rusting screwdrivers.

His dad must have been collecting these for ages. Every time he went down the Club. He never thought of his dad as crazy till this, just ignorant about his mam and John and himself. Though, to think of it, he had always spent too long in the bathroom. His mam often moaned about that.

Sam rummaged amongst them for paint, disturbing spiders who'd taken up residence in the tubes. Moving the watering-can which resembled an item from St. Fagan's Museum. He noticed two magazines folded up deliberately inside it. He pulled them out – *Penthouse.*

'The dirty bastard!'

He imagined his dad, collapsing onto a bed of bog-rolls, clutching a *Penthouse.* He resisted visualizing further scenes, conscious again of his own situation. The chase. On the run. His fingers felt among the water-weighted paper. Three tins at last: black, yellow and white. Brushes proved more elusive. Eventually, he tracked one down, sitting in the hutch next to a pink roll: an odd, stumpy creature.

On a shelf above were various tools in states of rusting and one old Stanley knife. Sam picked it up and weighed it in his hand, as if working out its worth. He pushed up the blade and tested it against his thumb. It was an insurance policy, that's all. You never knew when.

Through the estate, he was glad of twilight, darker because of cloud-covering. Everything appeared murkier. His smeared glasses caused that. A carrier full of paint and toilet-rolls. If the cops stopped him, they would wonder.

Penybryn was deserted, though he did discern a police-car in the distance and changed route, to take the path by the hospital next to the footie-field. Even with the safer sky and his dubious disguise, he was sure he'd be stopped. A few kids were kicking a ball round the field. It was a cross between rugby, football and karate as far as he could tell.

'Ey! Specky! What yew got in yewr bag? Gis a look!'

Sam looked around to see who their jibes were aimed at.

'Speck, speck, specky!

Give a little look to me!'

One of them did chicken impressions, running in Sam's direction. Sam was taken aback.

'Fuck off yew little twats!'

'Woah! Ark at Specsavers, eh!'

They hadn't expected his response. Took him for a wimp. A few years ago, he'd have been there with them. Not exactly playing footie, but messing about, having a laugh and waiting for someone to pass by to pick on. Now he wondered why he was doing this. For a girl who didn't really fancy him? For an empty flat soon to be knocked down?

He must be mad, like his dad. What was the use of paint? You couldn't drink it. Old, mouldering toilet-rolls in a shed. As the rain came down, his body was mud-heavy, just like them.

On the way back, he bought some water and a local paper. Water! He was getting really practical. They could actually wash now and try to get rid of the cloying smells.

As he entered the building, Sam was startled by a man approaching down the corridor from one of the lower flats. His first instinct was to do a runner, his second to act calm. He was caught between, like the still photo of someone about to leap.

The man looked dazed and bedraggled, but harmless enough. Sam thought he'd seen him down town, busking by the bus-station.

He was anxious to chat. 'They're gunna kick us out, y'know? Ey, yew livin upstairs? Didn know there wuz anybuddy there. They'll be comin soon! Wha's yewer name? I'm Will.'

'I'm...'

'D yew know, Princess Anne's visitin the estate? Yeah, maybe tha's why they wanna knock this lot down, or sell it an do it up. We got nowhere t go. Ow about yew?'

Will moved closer and closer to Sam, who could smell the lingering tobacco and weed on the man's floppy clothes. He was like a joint on legs, his hair like strands of dried leaves. Sam edged up the stairs.

'Look. I gotta go. See yew round, eh?'

Will seemed to register Sam for the first time, sense his anxiety.

'Don worry, I won' say nothin.'

'Yeh, thanks! I'll see yew.'

Sam hurried upstairs, half expecting Will to follow. He was disturbed by the encounter and the place seemed even less safe now. The way that young man with his unnaturally wrinkly face, talked so loosely, made him want to leave as soon as possible.

*

Shelly ignored his fears. She was more concerned about the fact that he'd returned with no red and a load of second-hand toilet-rolls! She showed him her fountain sketch.

'What is tha? Looks jest like a loada doodles t me!'

'This is a blood fountain. Blood's usually red. We need red paint!'

Sam paced up and down, hungry, sopping and not amused.

'I don bleeve yew! There's a bloke downstairs could grass us up. An all yewr bothered bout is the bleedin colour.' Then he stabbed a remark, 'Ewse yewr own blood! Yew got plenty of it!'

Mary manoeuvred between them like a boxing umpire.

'Whooaah! The Fugitive Three, member? That wuz below the belt, Sam!'

Shelly was about to pounce, when suddenly she saw humour in Mary's comment and a crooked-toothed grin cracked her face like a stone to ice.

After food (crisp butties had never tasted better) and water, Shell read the paper. She browsed through the first few pages, recalling some of the names in the column 'Look Who's Been In Court!' Her eyes fixed on the headline "Local Man In Drowning Tragedy". As she read on, she muttered to herself, 'Fuck, fuck, fuck, fuck...' and shook her head.

Mary and Sam both asked her the matter, but she just kept on reading till she slammed her fist down on the rotten table and it shuddered as if ready to collapse.

'I coulda done summin! I shoulda stayed with im that night. I woz a total ewseless fuckin coward!'

'What? 'Mary implored, 'what is it, Shell?'

'It's im... Clive... it's this bloke I met down town,

the same night I met yew, Sam. Ee's on'y drowned isself, tha's all.'

'Maybe it woz an accident, Shell. Yew ardly knew...'

'No way, Sam! We gotta do summin. We gotta make summin down town t remember im by... I mean, they put up statues to famous boxers an tha, s why not people like im?'

'Yeah, we'll do summin.'

'Don take the piss, Sam! The wall-paintin's jest the first...'

'I'm not takin...'

'I fuckin blew it, didn I? If on'y I'd-a lissened.'

Shelly went over again and again that night she met Clive. The drink, the tablets he was taking. How he needed someone to speak to. It had to be a sculpture. It must be made of old cans and grass: a clump at the top. While the others tried to comfort her, Shell was miles in the sky, shaping a memorial in her head.

As she sped along the pavements of Penybryn pushed by Shelly, Mary felt a sense of release. Shell wished she could share the emotion, but thoughts of Clive stalked her, just as she believed he had done that first evening.

For Mary, it belonged to the fleeting quality of their situation. It couldn't last, she knew, and that made their brave efforts to bring colour to the dull estate all the more worthy. For a while, she even forgot the comforts of her home: her warm bed, video and telly. Shelly let her free-wheel downhill and she whooped with delight, a small child at first sight of the sea. Sam pranced in front, as she clung to pots and brush under the blanket. They all seemed manic and free, as if the grubby flat never existed.

Shelly raced alongside her. 'Don crash Mare, or we

110

will ave real blood t paint with!'

Sam did a dervish swirl. 'See, I tol yew Shell, it's all part o my great plan!'

Eventually, they reached the shops and the exact spot where she'd come yesterday. But yesterday seemed like centuries away. She was a different person now. Changed forever.

Had she dreamt it, or was it in a photo? Her mam pushing her in a pushchair along Porthcawl prom, a huge ice-cream cone in her face. Her dad tut-tutting at her mess. Her mam laughing him aside. Mary's white face like a clown's make-up melting.

'Shell? Why ave we come yer?'

'Yew'll find out.'

He dug his hand under Mary's blanket.

'Ey, watch out!'

'C'mon, I know wha yew got idin under there!'

He produced a can of lager from among the paint cans, raising it like a team captain with a trophy.

'See, I think o evrythin!'

The rain had stopped and the sky was clearing into one of those Spring nights when anything seems possible. Sam thought of Art in school. Old Mrs Price tearing up his painting in front of the whole class. Throwing the pieces into the bin.

'Shell, what we doin? Yewr boss.'

'Jest lissen. We got yellow right? We'll do this wall yer, jest by where we found Mary. It's gonna be flames like a Phoenix fire and then there's these white things comin outa the flames, they'll look like pills but in fact they'll be UFOs. An right at the top a pair o knickers in the sky, like God's all-seein eye.'

'Yewr fuckin loopy!'

'That's brill, Shelly! It's like I've bin abducted by aliens. Which I ave in a way!' said Mary.

'Ey, oo yew callin a fuckin Martian?'

Sam placed his lager-can on his head and bleeped at the other two.

'Take me to yewer leader!'

'Yeah, tha's me! Now give us an and with this yellow. Really big flames, comin up like tongues.'

'Tongues, eh? Sounds good t me. Do I get t do the knickers?'

'Yew always get t do the knickers, Sam.'

Then Mary sat back and directed operations. Sam was happy to be bossed by the other two. Though wary at first, he followed Shelly's broad brushstrokes with an old brush they'd found in the flat. Nothing was certain except the original idea. He made his own fire leap high.

So the wall, which had previously been drab and scrawled with diverse graffiti, caught fire. In the place where Mary had almost died, the heat licked upward. In the growing dusk, it was as if the sun had come back to put its signature there.

'Jest a bit igher I'd say,' suggested Mary.

'Tha's what they always say!' quipped Sam, and Shelly ruffled his hair to tease.

The two wall-artists stood back to admire their work. Sam couldn't believe what they'd achieved. A touch of colour to dreary Pen, like planting flowers that couldn't be trodden on or stolen.

'Mind, it's getting nippy... Wish it woz a real fire!'

Shelly knew he was prouder than he was letting on. Next the pills. They had to resemble Paracetemol. Transform the further away they flew.

'Lemme ave a go first.'

'Oh, ark at Leonardo!'

112

'De Caprio, yew mean!' said Mary, surprising herself with the lightness of her comment.

Shelly found it hard at first to fashion the shape, making it three-dimensional. It kept looking like a disk.

'It don matter, tha's near enough!'

'Course it matters! Fuck it! I carn get it right!'

In her frustration, Shelly sprayed white paint at Mary, splattering her blanket.

'Yew tryin t make me into a Jackson Pollack?'

'Oh ho, lissen t Miss Swotty-Pants. Oo the fuck is Jackson Bollocks anyway?' Sam mocked Mary, but they all laughed in a gibboning chorus.

Shelly searched around the littered ground and scooped up a piece of rusted metal. She attempted to write 'Aspirin' on the white pill.

'Aspirin's shorter!' she explained and Mary resisted a comment on so much for artistic reality, wary of Sam's scathing.

With the metal stick, Shell shaded, creating depth. She possessed a natural talent which had never been nurtured at school. Mary could see she could have gone on to do art, but all those days missed from bunking can't have helped.

'Tha's it!'

'Really great, Shell!' Mary enthused.

'We carn do tha f evry one, it'll take ages!' Sam protested.

'Look, yew do the UFOs up the top an I'll do the pills changin inta them.'

'Ow do I reach up there?'

'Easy, yew balance on Mary's wheelchair.'

'I cun old onto is legs.'

'Oh great! I get all the easy jobs, don I?'

*

She couldn't sleep. The whiff of paint from her hands kept replaying the picture on the wall and Sam's ridiculous attempt at knickers with one large eye in their crotch. Her mind sped like the wheels of Mary's chair downslope. A sculpture on the very spot where she once lived, a tower like a rocket but constructed from broken bricks and rubble.

The hardness of the bath brought her back. It couldn't last. It never did. Sam would return to his mam. Mare to her comfort.

She heard him fumbling towards the bathroom again. He pushed the door and apologized.

'Sorry Shell, I gotta ave a burst.'

Black paint clung to his face in inky blotches. There was enough light from the full moon for her to watch him as he pissed. She could see his prick was enlarged. He had changed towards her, his tone apologetic, almost tender. He had joined her, knowing fully the risks he was taking.

'Ey, Sam. Come over yer, will yew?'

'Wha?' he said, expecting to be teased.

'Come over yer mun!'

She propped herself up in the bath. He was putting it away, politely zipping up.

'Wha's up, Shell?'

His face was child-like, as though he was about to be scolded. Shelly felt so generous towards him and he looked so comical there, like a miner covered in dust.

'Yew got some paint on yewr ol boy. I seen it.'

'Shut up! Stop takin the piss!'

'Don be stewpid, jest come over!'

He stood looking awkward, unsure of her next move. Shelly reached towards his zip and slid it down. He groaned a sigh of utter disbelief.

'Shell, yew don ave…'

'Jest shut up Sam, yew might put me off!'

It was something she'd never done before. In the past, boys always forced the pace. But this was for him: it was a gift.

She pulled out his prick and it was already moist at the tip. She held it firm in both hands, moving it up and down as Sam closed his eyes. He began to move his hips with her motion, as she rubbed with her palms. Low rounded sounds came from within him and Shelly still teased with her fingertips and her voice.

'No black paint yer, jest white!'

He held her face and kissed her hard, their tongues meeting like rapid brushstrokes. When he came in her hands, they both half-laughed and half-cried together in relief and wonder. Then he fell back onto the floor, overcome.

'Shell, I didn even know yew fancied me like tha.'

She held her head back.

'Course I do, Sam.'

'Cun I join yew in-a bath then?'

'Don be so darft, there's no room. We cun do more soon, eh?'

'Yeah, I carn wait!'

He kissed her again, full-lipped and eager. She stretched out, content. Maybe nothing, maybe something. It was impossible to predict.

Mary woke to intense heat. The full moon turned to full sun. She felt claustrophobic. A hostage, through her own choosing. She'd made her Hamlet-decision, but it hadn't been conscious. Something deep-down indefinable had said, 'to be.'

Now the sun beat rhythms of, 'Outside! outside!' The cracks and bareness of the miserable room were made worse by her craving for a shower, to wash away the smells of sweat and paint.

As she struggled to haul herself up from the wheelchair, she could hear small cries of pain coming from the kitchen. Nearing the door, the cries turned out to be Sam singing. She crept along and saw Sam shaking a cereal box like a percussion instrument. Then Shell came into view and Sam caught hold of her waist and began to nibble at her ear-lobe like a mouse at a tit-bit. Mary recoiled.

Everything had changed. They were no longer the Fugitive Three. She felt excluded. She was angry now; not with Shelly or Sam, but with Anthony and her father. She needed to confront them with her suffering. Make them realise what she'd been through.

She slipped away downstairs before they could detect. Their giggles followed her, making her more determined. She didn't want to desert her new-found friends, nor did she want to intrude on their love-play. Shell and Sam, who would have thought? She had wondered about Shelly, the way she'd stroked her hair and kissed her cheeks. Not that she hadn't enjoyed such attention.

Before the main door, she reached a window with a view of the grassy area outside. She saw them about twenty yards away and immediately ducked, like a soldier behind a parapet.

Her father, business-like and earnest as ever, in conversation with another man. Her initial reaction was that they were on her trail, the man a private detective of some sort. She took a peek. He was unconventionally dressed, with a Stetson hat and open-necked, multi-coloured shirt. He wore what seemed to be cowboy boots. Not exactly her dad's usual business colleague.

She thought of surrendering. She would emerge waving a white tissue, except she didn't have one. Maybe her dad had learnt. Maybe he would embrace his runaway daughter muttering I'm so sorry, love.

Despite last night, he still felt frustrated. She teased him and that made him unsure. She loved the power, but he didn't care. When he licked her ear, she joked.

'It's cleaner than them bowls now, I reckon! Why don yew lick them an all?'

He stopped singing because he thought he heard footsteps on the stairs.

'D yew yer summin?'

'Yeah, yew murderin Bob Marley!'

'Nah, I mean on-a stairs. I'd better check.'

He looked down the stair-well. Nothing. He went into the bedroom.

'Mary? Mare?'

The wheelchair was empty. No sign of her.

Panting back to Shelly – 'She've gone! Problee back t daddy. She'll say we kidnapped er. We'll go down. I bloody knew it!'

Shelly held both his hands, as if she was going to dance, smoothing them with her thumbs.

'Cool ead, Sam! She've mos likely gone f'r a walk.'

'Gone f'r a walk? She've ardly bin outa that wheelchair f fuck's sake! I don trust er.'

'Orright, if it makes yew appy, le's go an find er.'

They stepped downstairs hurriedly, finding Mary squatting below a large window.

'Mary! What woz yew…'

She shshed them with finger to lips and pointed up at the window. Sam was first there and, as he peered out, Mary grabbed him and pulled him down. He caught a glimpse of Castleton talking to a suit.

'Oh shit!'

Shell edged towards the window, expecting the police. Instead, it was Ray Gun and a posh-looking man. Castleton appeared to stare in their direction and she sat on the bottom step.

'It's my dad,' Mary whispered, 'but I don know the other guy. Maybe ee's a private dick.'

'A fuckin public dick more like!' Sam hissed.

'Oo is ee?' asked Mary.

'On'y Castleton. On'y the bloke oo tried t rape Shelly. Wha the ells yewr ol man doin botherin with im?'

Shelly sidled up to the window again and eyed out. She could see them walking away deep in conversation. She was relieved that Castleton had no heavies with him and that they weren't going to enter the flats.

Mary's mouth was still agape and she shook her head.

'They're goin away. We're orright... f now at least.'

Sam grasped Mary as though arresting her. She shoved him away.

'Leave off, will yew?'

The three stood away from the window.

'So ow come yew woz leavin without tellin us, eh?' Sam interrogated.

'Leave me alone, will yew? Yew don rule my life an I ope yew never rule ers!' Mary blurted out and immediately felt guilty.

Sam was about to retaliate with a put-down, but Shelly intervened.

'C'mon yew two, le's talk about it! Le's sit down an work it out.'

*

118

The glaring hot sky drew the stench out of the pipes and into the flat. Sewage mixed with cloying paint in a nauseating cocktail.

Sam sat against a wall fidgeting with his fingers, in need of a fag. Mary was slumped again in the wheelchair sporadically sobbing and offering excuses. Only Shell was focussed, scheming. She knew they had to get out, or they'd end up fighting. She also knew they all needed to be paid back: Mary's ex and her dad and that rat-on-two-legs Castleton. Now there was actually some connection between Mary's father, the upright Councillor and factory-owner and this shady landlord, it made revenge all the more necessary.

'Mare, stop blubberin an lissen up! What could ee ave bin doin with yewr dad… Ray Gun?'

'I dunno! My dad's chair of Ousin. Ee's in the Mason's. Any elp?'

'They're all fuckin crooks!' Sam cut in.

'Jest remember oos card yew ad in yewr pocket, Sam baby, before yew make out so great. Now, ousin – that sounds promisin. These flats peraps. Maybe Castleton's gonna take em over or summin?'

Mary gazed up from her sniffing, wishing she could think on her feet like Shelly.

'Yeah, I think that could be it! They get private landlords to take people in…'

'See ow many ee cun cram into is seedy B an B's, before they knock it all down,' Shelly continued the thread.

'Anyway, I int angin round t find out, we gotta leg it quick.'

Sam was impatient as ever, 'I don like tha Ray Gun sniffin round yer. Yew an me could go t Cardiff, Shell. Maybe even London.'

Mary stood up, the tightness of Shelly's clothes

digging into her, constricting her breath. She was determined. She had caught Shelly's sense of purpose.

'Cardiff? London? Ow about New York, eh? Fuck off, Sam! We got a job t do, even if it's the las thing we do t gether.'

This was Shelly and Mary's plan and it could all end in disaster. They had discussed it, but Sam had complained, not trusting Mary now she'd tried to escape. Sam had mocked their ideas, wanting a solution much more violent. It was typical of girls to come up with such a lame scheme, he'd said. But it suited them both and would be some sort of revenge.

She was out at last into the uncommonly warm estate. She had a sense of being followed. Sam? Her disguise was totally inadequate: Shell had lopped her hair off, claiming she was an expert and had done all the haircuts in the homes. Sam called her a female Sid Vicious and Shell said it was about time for a punk revival.

For the first time since her suicide attempt, there was optimism in her stride. If Sam wanted to follow, so what? Hopefully, her dad wouldn't return home. She pressed the key in her hand till it hurt. Just ahead, she stopped dead at a siren, but it was an ambulance speeding up the road.

She seemed to float downhill now. She was light-headed and dizzy from lack of food and sleep. Despite that, the future nagged. She wanted to be like Shelly, playing out the moments.

No car in the drive. When she let herself in, she felt like a burglar. She noticed a woman's coat on the stand and wondered if she'd already moved in to take her mam's place. She felt cheated. She hated him for that;

carrying on with his life when she was missing.

She crept around like a stranger, expecting to be startled any second by that Dorothy. But every room was empty, though her dad's bed was unmade. She examined it for signs, even sniffed in disgust at the smell of a woman's perfume clinging to the pillows, a pollution cloud.

She had to act quickly. By the phone a list of numbers. There was Ant's and also the hospital. So he was on her trail. Perhaps the meeting with that landlord did have something to do with her, not a business deal?

She had to get the order right. Ant wouldn't be in. She'd leave a message. He might not turn up. It was worth the risk. Better still, his mother answered.

'Oh Mary, I'm so glad to yer yew. They sayd yew'd bin taken up the ospital an then gone missin. I tol Anthony. Ee've bin appallin. Ee must apologize.'

'Mrs Pearson, please! Please! I'm okay! But I do need t see im urgent. If ee's a real man then ee'll meet me. Up the Arches, nine o'clock t night. Please tell im t be there. '

'The Arches? Mary, yewr not goin to do summin crazee I ope? The Arches, I mean.'

'No, Mrs Pearson, I promise I won'. I jest wanna see im somewhere really quiet. Tell im it's really important. Okay?'

'I will, love. I'll make shewer, even if I ave to drag im up there myself!'

'Thanks, Mrs Pearson! An don worry, right?'

'Yes, love. Take care!'

She was almost certain he'd come. His mother would badger him. He'd think she intended to jump, or threaten to.

Castleton next. A difficult one. She was no actress,

121

but could fake a posh accent, Joanna Lumley style.

'Yes, what is it?' he sounded breathless, flustered.

'It's Councillor Croft's personal secretary.'

'What? I woz on'y talkin to im a while ago. Wha's up?'

'Well. He says something very important has cropped up and he must meet you tonight.'

'T night? Dunno if I cun make it, love.'

'It really is vital.'

'Der, yew don give up, d yew? Will yew be there?'

Mary gulped back a giggle.

'No, I'm afraid not sir.'

'Where to?'

'He says he wants to meet you… up the Arches.'

'The Arches? Why the ell…?'

'Perhaps he wants to discuss the development of housing in that area with you, sir.'

'Eh? This is all a bit weird, yew ask me! What time?'

'9 pm precisely he said.'

'Yew mus be takin the p… Yew mus be avin a larf. Nine o'clock at night up the Arches?'

Mary thought she was losing him. She thought he was suspicious.

'It's most important, sir!' She began to sound machine-like, but she was desperate. 'I think he said he wants to conclude the deal as soon as possible.'

It was a risk. There might be no deal. She could've blown it!

'Really? Oh, orright then. Tell im I'll be there. Jest coz yewr so persuasive, love. Yew sound like that woman off-a telly tha…'

'Thank you, Mr Castleton!'

'S long, love!'

It was all going well. Something was bound to go wrong. Next her dad. She had to be super-quick as he'd trace it and be back in a flash. Worse still, send the police.

She went into the lounge carrying the cordless. Fell back into her favourite chair and was tempted to doze off She was so exhausted. A copy of her Emily Dickinson lay on the coffee-table, where she'd abandoned it, unable to concentrate, anxious about Ant what seemed so long ago. She picked it up and skimmed through, even though time pressed. She came to a poem which summed up her last few days –

The heart asks pleasure first

And then, excuse from pain-

It ended with "The privilege to die". Well, she'd had that particular 'privilege', but been re-born. Now she felt more her old self, confident enough to talk silently to her mam's presence in the house.

'Mam, I'm so sorry. I've gotta make summin of my life f yew. I know yew'd want that. Not what I done. I'm really sorry, mam!'

If only there was a line to the beyond. A secret number.

Mary tried his office, but he wasn't in. She dialled his mobile, her breath stuttering.

'Hello, Frank speaking. Is that you, Dorothy?'

Mary couldn't summon up a response. The home number must have come up.

'Hello? Is anything wrong?'

'Dad!'

'Mary, it's you! Are you alright? I've been so worried! They said someone of your description had been brought into the Prince of Wales, but with a different name. Where have you been? What happened? I've had the police out…'

'Dad!'

'Yes…You're home! I'm so glad you've come back. '

123

'Dad, lissen! I'm not back yet! I'm stayin with frens. Don't worry!'

'What do you mean, you're not back?'

'I'm safe. We mus meet. Tonight. Up the Arches. Nine o'clock. I promise not t mess yew about in future if yew jest meet me there. Please Dad?'

'The Arches? Do you mean the viaduct? Why up there for goodness sake? You're not planning anything…'

'Dad! Jest f once. Do what I say, an evrythin will be orright!'

'Oh, okay! I don't know what's going on, but I'll do it to please you. Though I can't see why you can't just stay at home. Dorothy will be there in a jiff.'

'The Arches. Nine o'clock. See yew, Dad!'

She pressed red. Dorothy, not him. Even now, he was probably thinking about meetings. The police had been searching, but not him. He'd been out with that crook Ray Gun planning to demolish the place where she happened to be staying. The large ball could have hit it, sending the whole flats tumbling. She could've been buried in the debris and then he'd have to take notice.

The three men would get it, right between the eyes. Fountains of red as Shelly had prophesied.

Everest, Snowdon, Pen-y-fan, Ben Nevis, Sugar Loaf…Whoever named these streets after mountains was a joker. Unlike the mountains, most streets were identical, like the factory-lines or superstores many worked in. Without Shelly's vision, Sam wouldn't have seen these things. It was like looking at the estate for the first time, even though he'd always lived here.

They never seemed to ask the people who actually

lived here what they wanted, no matter who was in power. And Shelly just wanted to do her bit to change their environment, however small the mark she made.

Some families attempted to make a difference: build a wall, have a patio. But what was it but a few bricks and bushes? It all seemed pointless, when crime and drugs dragged you down and people only worked to survive, a few luxuries along the way.

He was startled out of this rare thoughtful state by a car pulling up opposite. He was almost home and, though he didn't recognise the driver, he began to power-walk. The car turned with a screech and slowed down alongside him. Window down. Milky's head, large shades and baseball cap.

'Ey, knicker-boy!'

Sam was taken aback.

'Oose car? Is it skanked?'

'Nah, my ol man's. Le's mule it! C'mon eh?'

'Nicked it off yewr ol man more like.'

'Anyway, talkin of nickin...'

'Yeah, I'm really sorry, Milky. Onest!'

Sam angled into his pockets. Amazingly, they were still there. He hooked out Shelly's black knickers and offered them to his friend.

'Yer, Milk, ave a sniff! I think yew'll agree these are prime fish. The business, mun!'

'Bloody ell, Sam. Yew do ave a collection! Keep yewr knickers to yewrself. Look, yew comin or wha? We could go up-a Red Cow, ave a few pints. I could tell yew about Mel an make yew dead jealous.'

'Nuh, sorry Milk! I'm busy! Another time. Once I'm sorted.'

Sam went close to the car-door now. He was glad his friend bore no grudge. Milky suddenly recalled something and looked worried.

'Ey Sam, yew orright? '

'Ow d yew mean?'

'Well, we wuz up-a Royal las night an these two blokes come in lookin f yew. They looked really rock, ex-bloody Para's or summin. Yew in trouble?'

'Oh fuck! No, I better go. Lissen, yew aven seen me right? An if yew ave seen me then I woz jest off t Cardiff, or London.'

'Make that New York!'

'Wha?'

Weird. Like *déjà vu*, he thought.

Getting home he had no key and his dad answered the door. It wasn't even mid-day, but he stank of booze. His face was blown-up and his eyes swimming. Soon they would drown.

'Where've yew bin, Sam an wha's this about a job? I ope yewr bringin some money ome.'

'Dad, I jest gotta collect summin. I wuz back a while ago, got some paint from-a shed.'

By now they were in the sitting-room and his dad collapsed into a chair with a groan of pain.

'Don tell er, will yew son? She'll think I'm goin loopy!'

'Tha's orright, dad. Yew collect bog-rolls an I collect these!' He waved the black knickers in front of his dad. 'So we really ave got summin in common.'

'Bloody ell, Sam! Yewr gettin a proper perve!'

'Not really, dad, I jest collect thins. It's a good thing I do, coz I'm yer for some Allowe'en masks.'

'Wha? Yew goin to rob a bank or summin?'

'If on'y, dad. If on'y!'

Sam was the guide, but Shelly knew the way. In the carriers was all their equipment. She'd used the last of

Mary's money. Sam had come up trumps with the masks and hoodies. Mary walked now; the wheelchair would be far too awkward. Shelly didn't know if there was any future for them after this. She still bled, though less gushing and she felt stronger as they tramped on. The sun was moving westward onto their backs as they veered over the main road and along the country road past the old TB Sanatorium.

'I ewsed t go f'r picnics down yer, but I aven been this way f'r ages,' Mary explained.

'I never knew any of this woz yer till I wen with boys off the estate. I seen a lot of the sky arfta that.'

Sam had a stick and was lopping the heads off various grasses with it. He was in his element.

'We woz smokin blow up-a Golf Course once. Crashed out in-a bunker when this ball lands right nex to us. Milky puts it in is mouth an when this golf guy comes along ee challenges im t it it from where it landed, right from is gob!'

'Did ee?'

'Nuh, went t phone-a cops. Sayz we wuz trespassin.'

Mary hopped in front of the others, walking backwards to get attention. To Shelly, she seemed all the more attractive with her prickly haircut and dark eyes squinting in the sun.

'So where yew goin arfter t night, Shell? Sam?'

'Same as yew!' quipped Sam.

'Where's that?'

'Prison!'

'It int that bard, is it?' said Shelly.

'No, seriously.'

'I dunno.'

'Nor me.'

'So what if I said I woz goin ome?' asked Mary.

'Tha's no problem!' replied Sam.

But Shell was disappointed. She thought Mary needed her more than that. How could she return to a father who conspired with the likes of Ray Gun?

'But yewer dad…Yew said ee didn give a toss bout yew. Even when yew phoned im…'

'I know, Shell, I know. But…'

Mary sniffed herself under her armpits.

'I'm desperate f'r a shower!'

'Oh, ark at Miss Poshy-pants, eh?' Sam mocked, 'an anyway, pretty soon, yewr wish will be my command, or whaever.'

Shelly glared at him and he was confused by her sullen manner.

'Mary! Maybe we cun take over somewhere else? Some ol farm an live…'

'Off the fatta the lan'!' Mary said, *'Of Mice and Men'* and laughed.

'Don take the piss!'

'No, Shelly, I never meant to…it's from a book.'

'We could live off·grass!' Sam announced, pulling up some wild rye and chewing it.

'Wha's wrong with tha? I once met this bloke down town oo swore ee ate nothin but grass.'

'Smoked it, more like!'

The narrow road wound, like a meandering stream, down to the valley bottom. It seemed a thousand miles from Penybryn estate with its people struggling for light in a world which heaped darkness upon them. Yet, it was only a walk away and Sam knew it well from days of wandering.

'Jest down there's a ewge log over-a river. We ewsed t dare each other t run across real fast. Once I slipped an fell in! I musta bin on'y bout ten an the others all pissed theirselves while I woz strugglin. The water woz rushin an it wuz ard t get t the bank. In the end, my yellin musta scared the shit outa them, coz they got a big branch an managed t fish me out! My mam didn arf give me a bollickin when I got ome drippin wet. I wuz grounded f'r a week.'

They came to the single-lane bridge and a car passed them very carefully. Its middle-aged male driver examined them closely, as if taking mental notes.

'Bloody ell. Is ee CID or wha?'

'Don be so fuckin paranoid!' said Shelly.

As they clambered over the stile and onto the footpath which skirted the river, Mary was awe-struck by the place. She recalled only a grassy area and the over-towering viaduct which lay further up the valley. She was amazed by this powerful little river which cut so deeply into rocks and the blacky-brown pool below they called Blue Pool.

'We're not goin in-a Blue Pool then?'

'No chance, too close to-a road,' said Sam.

'We'll afto make shewer we ide the stuff while we're swimmin.'

'No worries, Shell. Where we're goin few men ave ever trod. Not even David fuckin Attenbro!'

Out of the estate, Shell felt more helpless. She'd only ever come here when drunk, with the likes of Leon Jones, Sam's old mate. Then, all the countryside had merged into one: woods and animal noises in a cauldron, like the punch-bowl of a waterfall. Once she'd been abandoned by this boy. He'd had his way and then dumped her. Her mam wouldve mocked her – 'What, yew mean yew never even nicked his wallet? Yew are a muppet!'

Sam caught her waist, noticing her change.

'Wha's up Shell? It int like yew t be so sad.'

She wriggled him off instinctively, the memory of 'users' still fresh.

'Ey, c'mon, take a chill pill!'

'Where we goin Sam?'

'Jest up-a valley. I know a lovely spot.'

As they walked under the Arches, Mary couldn't believe how suddenly the landscape altered and the river-banks widened to a grassy plateau. The place of her family picnic, she was certain. She imagined herself sitting on a large boulder dangling her feet in the water, her mam arranging all the sandwiches and cakes. She must have been very young, because even her dad had been more playful then, throwing stones into the river and echoing their sounds for her.

As they progressed up valley, the footpath became harder to negotiate. Despite the sunlight, it was very slippery in shady parts and once Mary nearly lost her footing, grabbing Sam and almost dragging him down slope.

'Sorry Sam, I'm not ewsed to walking.'

Light pierced through gaps in the canopy, a sharp sky spurring them on. Whenever the river ran westward it was a bright slide.

'Ow far, Sam?' asked Shelly.

'Neally there now… It'll be worth it. This place is special. Yew wait!'

'Ow did yew discover it, Livingstone?' asked Mary.

'Amazin wha yew find on-a magies, see. Actually, maybe we woz trippin… maybe we magined the whool thin.'

Shell gave Sam a push, this time teasing. He made out to fall from the path, but clutched an overhanging branch and began to make monkey-noises.

Then, all of a sudden, the valley opened up. There before them was a small yet fast-flowing waterfall, with a pool under it and gravelly beaches by the river. Shell and Mary stood captivated; the sky came down on this spot and most of the clear pool was alive with sunlight.

Sam hopped down onto the pebbly crescent with a smug expression. 'See, I tol yew! Epic or wha?'

He lodged his carrier with weighty stones and began to strip off.

'Care t join me f'r a swim, ladies? Or will that be a shower, madam?'

He gestured to Mary, indicating the fall with its white-bubbling gush.

'Wow!' Mary exclaimed.

Shelly observed Sam, so at home, so natural: his bony, wiry body all energy here. Mary laughed as he bared himself so quickly, revealing a pair of black knickers he was wearing under jeans.

'I wore these specially f yew, Shell!'

He did a mock-strip for the girls, chanting the accompaniment – 'Duh dum dum, da duh dum dum. De-rum, de-rum…'

With his back to them, he wiggled out of the knickers, tripping and landing face first on the stones. He held his face and moan-groaned.

Shelly knew better, but Mary scampered over, concerned. As soon as she reached him, he leapt up, grabbed her and swung her towards the pool. She was up to her knees and staggering, spluttering giggles.

'Right!' shouted Shell. 'This means war!'

She dived onto the small beach, leaving her carrier near Sam's. She retrieved her knickers from the ground and tried to pull them over his head. He struggled as Mary splashed him with water.

'Leave off, Shell!'

'C'mon, Mare! Give us an and!'

They attempted to grasp his arms, but he was slippery as a trout. In all the excitement, he became hard and erect. Shelly noticed it and slipped the

131

knickers from his head, only to hook them onto his prick, so it resembled a flag-pole with black flag. Mary fell back, overcome by laughter, while Sam jumped into the pool to hide his predicament. Shell's machine-gun laughs brought showers of freezing spray onto the two girls from Sam.

'Fuckin ell, it's brass monkeys!'

Shelly soon stripped off and was urging Mary to follow suit.

'I've never bin skinny-dippin, it's a bit…'

'Don be darft, yew wan tha shower, don yew? Yew got nothin t be ashamed of. Look at me, one boob bigger than the other an a lovely scar from an operation by yer. C'mon, Mare, join the fun!'

Reluctantly, Mary began to undress. The water seemed so inviting, especially below the waterfall itself. As Shell waded in gingerly, unsteady on the uneven rocks of the river-bottom, Mary was delighted to rid herself of the tight-fitting clothes. But down to bra and pants she sat and hugged herself, still thinking of the dream she'd had and how vulnerable she'd felt being naked. She smiled as the others cavorted like a couple of dolphins. Shelly looked over.

'Okay, Mary, yew don come in, we got no choice, ave we Sam?'

'Too true!'

They were approaching her, making grunting noises like monsters from the deep. It was like they were all children again and their mood was infectious. She sprang back onto the grassy bank.

'No way!'

As she backed off, Sam did a rugby tackle on her right leg, bringing her down. Shelly grabbed one arm and Sam the other. She couldn't shake them off, all the time yelling in mock-hysteria.

'Let me go! Let me go!'

They dripped water all over her and marched her towards the pool, like a citizen's arrest.

'Right, Mare, this is it!'

'In yew go, lovely girl!'

She was flung into the pool and fell, face down in the shallow water. Its cold brought screams from her, so she bobbed up and down to get warm. Sam dived at her, hands like tentacles at her pants and bra.

'Orright, Sam, give over will yew?'

She slid off the knickers and unclipped her bra with great difficulty, due to numb hands. She threw them onto the shingle. Now that she felt loose and free the cold didn't matter. She was a strong swimmer and a few strokes took her to the waterfall. Underneath it she was swept downward, but came up again for the white torrent, plastering her hair and beating against her skin, the river's inner rhythms. This was the moment she was truly alive again, not some invented person and not even the Mary of old, who'd lived for Anthony.

Oblivious to Mary, Shelly and Sam were playing and joking, Shell with her legs gripped around his waist.

'Cor, bloody ell, Shell. If on'y...'

'I jest ope this Tampax olds out, or yew'll be drinkin my blood!'

'Tasty! Bit like black puddin I reckon.'

'Anyway, it's a lot lighter now.'

'Could we?'

'Shut up Sam! Oo, wha's that lump o rock down there?'

She poked one hand under the surface.

'Oh Shell! Mary wouldn know. She's far away, gettin showered.'

'Sam mun. Jest wait, eh? It'll be worth it – like this place.'

He sat down in the shallow with her astride him. They kissed deep and long and both knew that it wasn't only the spring sun, the mountain pool and their nakedness: it was something else. Neither had experienced it before. They daren't call it a name, for fear of losing it. Everything Shelly had ever had she had lost and Sam had only ever seen girls as bodies to be explored and conquered. The silence was theirs and they shared it.

Mary was bored. She wished they'd said eight rather than nine. She thought she could understand those soldiers in World War I. She had read Pat Barker. The tedium must have been interminable, so no wonder they'd tried to get 'Blighty wounds' to send them back home. It was fifteen minutes to go and the other two were canoodling as though in a nest, whispering so she felt left out.

All the possible mishaps nagged her now, like the rustling of animals in the woods behind them. What if her dad and Castleton actually met before the viaduct? What if Ant got scared and failed to turn up? At least she could rely on him being late, he always was. What if someone else came along the path over the Arches, some late evening dog-walker or courting couple?

'Ey Mare! Put yewr mask on! I cun see car lights up the top!' Sam hiss-called to her from behind a tree. As she attached her Dracula mask she felt like a real criminal, like she was about to mug someone, or worse.

The headlights were off and she could hear voices. Why voices? Luckily, it was a cloudless evening and she should be able to distinguish the figures as they came nearer. She could make out conversation before their silhouettes.

'I don't know. I just hope for your sake…'

'Mr Croft, I'm shewer she'll be orright. I'm sorry, I'm really…'

It was her dad and Anthony. Together! Now she could discern her dad's upright gait and Anthony bowing slightly to the shorter man. As they approached the middle of the viaduct, Sam was gesticulating at her wildly to hide herself. But they weren't focussed ahead and, instead, her dad stopped exactly half way across. He scanned around and she had to take refuge behind a trunk. She thought of *Macbeth* and Macduff's army at Dunsinane, each soldier camouflaged by a tree.

Her father's tones carried distinctly down the line of the old railway track.

'I hope she hasn't done anything stupid, I really do! I daren't look down. I'm sure she wouldn't. She's really a sensible girl. Or she used…'

'I'm shewer yewr right, Mr Croft. She wants t meet up, tha's all.'

She peeked again and saw more headlights from the car-park opposite the derelict pub. Shelly gave her a thumbs-up sign, like a captain ready to go over the top. She wanted to giggle at their disguises: Frankenstein's monster and a witch. Everything was working out as planned. Well, almost. But when Castleton appeared, they'd have to move rapidly, because he'd probably interpret it all as a mistake and leave her dad and Anthony there.

She thought about what Shelly had said: guerrilla artists bringing fountains of red! Sometimes Shelly could sound so intelligent for a girl who'd bunked off school so much.

Without thinking, she shook her can in readiness. It rattled.

'What was that, Anthony?'

'I dunno. It came from down there!'

She cursed herself, as Sam and Shelly raised their fists. At the same time, another voice boomed along from the other end of the viaduct.

'Ey, Councillor Croft! Wha's appnin? Oo's this with yew?'

She was terrified and thrilled at the same time. One raised palm from Shelly and that was it. Over the parapet. Maybe shot down. The tactics were simple: she'd go for Ant while Sam would attack her dad, so Shell could rush past and go for Ray Gun.

'Goodness me, what brings you here Castleton? Have you got anything to do with...'

The signal. Mary and Sam led the assault. They'd planned on silence, but Sam suddenly let out a banshee shriek which matched his disguise and Mary echoed it. They whole valley filled with their noise. Her father began to run. Anthony faced up. Castleton shouted something she couldn't make out.

Within seconds, she confronted Ant. She aimed the red paint for his face like a gun and he shielded himself. Sam was spraying her retreating father on the back, while Shell raced towards Castleton.

In all the commotion, they could just hear him yelling, 'Boyz! Urry up!'

Shelly was fountaining red over Castleton's flapping body, when two men came running downhill from the car-park. One threw himself on her, soon overpowering her. The other flew towards Sam, who pulled something out of his jeans pocket. The burly man stopped dead.

'Ey, ee've got a fuckin blade, Ray! Put that down, son, or yewll fuckin regret it.'

Castleton was wiping his face and moving in on Sam, who was yelling, 'Leave er go! Leave er go an I won urt no-one!'

Mary reacted quickly. Hauling herself up the wall of the Arches, she tore off her mask. Anthony recognised her first and looked shocked to see his attacker turn into his ex-girlfriend. One of Castleton's heavies, sitting on Shelly, ripped off the mask for their boss to inspect.

'Ey, Ray, look at this yer! Int she the bitch yewr arfta?'

Ray Gun glanced back as he circled round Sam.

'Yeh, I'll ave er arfter.'

They were about to pounce on him. Mary knew she must take control.

'Dad! It's me! Lissen. Yew'd better tell yewr friends to leave them alone. Dad! I'll jump! I've tried t take my life before an I cun do it agen! I'm tellin yew, Dad!'

Her father joined Anthony, equally stunned into silence. He gawped at his daughter in amazement.

'Dad, these are my bes frens. Either yew tell im t let them go or I bloody jump. An yew know I mean it. Yew know why I woz up-a ospital It's yewr choice!'

Her father edged towards her. She thought he was going to clasp her ankles.

'Mary, please! What is all this about? Why have you done this?'

For an instant, she gazed down the side of the viaduct. Even in the falling darkness she could sense the drop. The last thing she wanted. She wavered and almost fell the other way, onto the old track. With his jumper covered in red and with Ant's face smeared red they were both wounded animals and wounded animals were dangerous.

'I could do it, yew know I could... Tell im Dad! Tell im!'

'Go on, Mr Croft, please do as she sayz!' pleaded Ant.

Her dad shook his head in disbelief, but confronted Castleton.

'Ray, look, I know how you feel, but call off your dogs, will you?'

'Ey, less of the dogs!' moaned the heavy who pinned down Shell.

'Fuckin ell, Frank, yew need t sort yewr daughter out, yew ask me. She needs t find some tidee frens.'

He stared now at Sam, who pulled off his mask in a gesture of defiance. Castleton let out a sarcastic laugh.

'Fuckin ell, it's Knicker-Boy! Well, well… Ood-a thought! Yew shat on me, Knicker-Boy an I'll ave yew like I'll ave er. Jest a matter o time! Cmon boyz, let the rats crawl back inta theyr oles. We still gotta deal Frank, yeah?'

'Naturally Castleton! You'll keep quiet about all this I take it?'

'Dad! Yew gotta get im t promise ee never touches them agen. Ee's gotta leave them alone!'

'She owes me money, Frank. She done a runner without payin er rent. An the boy is jest a scumbag! I give im things an ee broke is word!'

'Yeah, an tell im ow yew tried t fuckin rape me, tha's all!' The other heavy muffled her too late.

'It's true, dad! It's true!' Mary cried.

'She's a fuckin liar, Frank!'

Mary stood up, on a tight-rope. She was wobbling and a strong breeze would have blown her over.

'Dad!'

'Right! Look, I'll pay you whatever she owes. Will you please guarantee that you won't pursue the matter? Ray? I want my daughter back!'

*

Sam spent ages preening himself. Every spike mattered, like a vain hedgehog. All he could imagine was him and Shelly naked and entwined in the pool. Shelly in that dreary flat handling him so expertly. Shelly, finally triumphant, with her own place on the estate. His dad hammered the bathroom door and he thought for a second about Ray Gun. Would he have any peace in this town any more?

'Bloody ell, Sam! What yew doin in there? Urry up, I'm bustin!'

Sam thought it was funny, the bogomaniac wanting him to get a move on. Passing his dad, he couldn't resist a comment.

'We're runnin outa bog-roll dad. Got any?'

'Leave it out, son!'

He couldn't keep his mind off her. She had forgiven him for the knife. At first she was really angry and accused him of trying to destroy her plan. He stopped himself from telling her how pathetic he thought the scheme was, with its spray-paint which should have been real blood.

He wanted to move in as soon as he could, but was scared she'd reject him. She still had plans to change the estate and he wasn't part of them. To him, it was pointless. Better to save and get out, move to a new estate up Blaenmorlais. He never thought he'd have such domesticated views. Shelly would be disgusted, would knock them down like those flats where they'd lived.

Downstairs, his mam was busy baking. Always a good sign. It meant a return to the old days: soft smells of the sponges of his childhood. It meant that his dad might even have promised to search for work, or maybe just that he wasn't going down the Club that night.

He breezed into the kitchen and she jumped.

'Sam, what's that pong? You smells like one o them hairems! Where you goin?'

'Downtown with Shelly. She's callin!'

'Ey, tell you what, you've changed!'

'I should think so, I bin wearin the same clothes all week!'

'Give over! No, you really are different.'

'C'mon mam, it's jest a date.'

But it was more. Avoid the Royal, they might get thrown out. They might meet up with Mary after that and it would be the three of them again. Runaways returned.

She was falling asleep still holding her Dickinson. So many poems and most discovered after her death. Her life fascinated Mary more than her work. Why the recluse? Mary brooded over a poem about a storm and 'Doom's electric Moccasin'. She imagined Emily obsessed with Red Indians, in a state of siege.

Then she was in a restaurant with her father and Dorothy. Strangely, Dorothy was wearing an Ascot-style hat, only instead of the usual quirky top, it had a skyscraper on it. Her dad was talking in Morse code, all 'Dot' this and 'Dot' that.

It was "Dine in a mine". She'd seen it in the local paper, but this was taking it too far! The cutlery consisted of small pick-axes and they had to eat out of butty-cans. The waiter was bare-chested and had a miner's helmet and lamp on his head.

Mary kept repeating, 'Dad, I carn take no more of this!' While he behaved bizarrely, ordering 'coke' and 'anthracite steak'.

Suddenly, Shelly and Sam burst in, clad in balaclavas

and holding large squeezy plastic tomatoes. She knew it was them because they squirted the red ketchup like paint all over the walls and guests, who retaliated by flinging their pick-axe knives and spade-like forks. Mary was jolted by a stray knife which struck her on the arm!

She opened her eyes with the shock. Her dad must've prodded her arm.

'Dad?'

'Hey, Mary! You were well away. Dorothy's coming over soon. Have you decided?'

She was still in a daze. Dreams, like poetry, were best left without interpretation. Yet, she had to analyze.

'Decided?'

'Yes! Don't you remember? I asked you out for a meal with myself and Dorothy. She so much wants to chat.'

He was still so formal, despite what had happened. But he'd been good to them, when he could've forgotten Shelly completely. Mary was back. Back to her books and a feeling that her Dad, for the first time since her mam died, actually cared about her. It had taken so much to do this. She had died and come back as Shelly. Shelly would always be with her.

Mary smiled. Her smile widened into a grin and she saw her father covered in tomato sauce looking flabbergasted, so her grin became a laugh, an uncontrollable monkeyish giggling as her dad stared in incomprehension.

'What?' he asked, 'What the devil is it?'

'Oh dad, it's jest a dream I ad tha's all. Yeah, I'd love to come with yew. As long as we don dine down a mine, that is!'

There were no shells. She'd meant to. Somewhere else perhaps. Her tag. Of course, somebody had spider-written right over their painting –

Kayleigh is a cock sukar.

Even she knew the spelling was wrong and it brought a toothy grin.

The flames were already fading, the UFOs resembled fried eggs and, as for Sam's knickers, they were more like a badly-drawn kite! Still, it was a beginning and there were so many walls and buildings to liberate.

It had happened so rapidly, she could hardly get her head round it. Mary's father had got her a flat and she was priority anyway, he said. Even so, she had resisted.

'It's a fix, Mare. I carn do it!'

'No way, Shell! Ee sayz yewr entitled. An anyway, yew've bin evicted by Castleton. Yew could even press charges, but my dad reckons yew don stand a chance. It's is word against yewers.'

Shelly knew she was right. Castleton had half the cops in his pockets. She accepted the offer knowing Ray Gun would never go away. He or his cronies would always be lurking and, even with Sam at her side, she could never really relax in Cwmtaff. He was like a satellite eye in the sky and no number of promises would reassure her that he wouldn't choose his moment to strike.

For now, it was another Saturday and she was going to Sam's. Heading on to pubs and clubs for the first time since she met him. Joining the throng from the estate, out to get hammered, to lose their heads. She kicked a lager-can and knew that soon she must collect.

She thought of that sculpture where her old house once stood, that rocket moulded out of the ruins of the

142

place where she'd suffered. The rocket became a syringe, but at its top, its needle-ending, there would be a single shell, a twirling, round white whelk: her signature, spiralling upwards to one sharp point.